Fine Old High Priests

Phyllis,

*How kind of you to call
me and invite me to
speak. I feel as though
i've gained a new friend.*
Best wishes,

Ann

Donald S. Smurthwaite

Bookcraft
Salt Lake City, Utah

All characters in this book are fictitious,
and any resemblance to actual persons,
living or dead, is purely coincidental.

Library of Congress Catalog Card Number: 98-74737
ISBN 1-57008-629-X

Printed in the United States of America   72082-2582

10   9   8   7   6   5   4   3

To all the fine old high
priests who have marked the way

CHAPTER ONE

Whether it is late winter or early spring, I cannot tell. I am older now, seventy-two in November, and beginnings seem much the same as endings. Seventy-two! Almost ancient, I should say. "You qualify for all the discounts now," my wife reminds me. "All of them. You are among the revered in our society." Little do I feel revered when a fast-food sandwich costs a quarter less than the price paid by a young man with four children in line behind me or when the senior space in the grocery store parking lot beckons coyly on cold January days. I do not feel honored at such times; I feel old.

But as other of life's pleasures become fleeting and fall away, I accept what age offers me: joy in small things, memories, and a measure of wisdom. It is the work of the old, this balancing of what leaves with the preciousness of what we can still hold close.

"All will be restored," Helen says. "All. The hairs on your head. No wrinkles or age spots. You will be in perfect physical condition with your mental capacity performing at its peak. I'd say about twenty-eight years old. That was you at your best."

So I remember that we all will be twenty-eight years old again sometime, and it comforts me a little, especially when things that are important start to slip away. "You remember when," my wife sometimes starts sentences. And I dread what comes next, because sometimes I do not remember when, or who, or what, or how, and faces become blurry and names unknown and my mind feels as though it stretches but never quite reaches any place.

And I fear that the stories of my life may not be remembered by me or anyone else.

So this is what it is like to be seventy-one, and, given all, aging is much overrated.

Not all is ebbing, though. I can still hit a golf ball straight and true down the fairway, though forty yards less than a decade ago. I still read Dostoyevsky and plink a tune on the piano. I can still hike in my mountains, mile after mile, for most of a day. I can still drive my car.

I am driving now. The road I travel leads west. Twilight swirls about me, shadows long and spindly. The sun sinks low against the February horizon, a thin line of cream, yellow, and gray. Clouds, dark blue and leaden, lie heavily upon the skyline. If I look closely along the roadside, Russian olives seem almost ready to burst into bud, allowing me to dream of a coming spring. If I remember the chill of the wind and how I pulled my coat higher as I left home a few moments ago, I realize that not all of the storms that blow hard and spit snow have yet passed.

My journey this yellow and gray evening is for a friend. He is still and frail, and his pale-blue eyes are most likely closed as he lies in his hospital bed. Samuel Nicholson soon will take a breath, let it escape, and breathe no more. His wife, Ruth, fears to leave his side, but fatigue shows in her face and crackles fray her voice and the strain is becoming more than she can bear.

"Can you . . . It is okay . . . Is it right of me to ask?" she says haltingly on the phone.

"Yes. Of course. You need to take care of yourself, Ruth. You've done all that can be expected. If anything changes during the night, I'll let you know. I can call you, then call Helen. She can pick you up and you will be here in twenty minutes. Please. I would like to. He won't be alone, and I know that is what you worry about."

She assents reluctantly, after a pause, and I'm sure a hundred thoughts pass through her mind in a lone second. "All right, Marcus. You can come. But I'll be back early. A few hours of sleep. I think that would help, and it's all I need."

And I am honored that she is willing to share some of these last, usually private moments and that I am the one who is entrusted with them.

I turn into the hospital parking lot, and because it is early evening when most people are at home or heading there, soon to sit at a table for dinner, I have little trouble finding a parking space.

I pull my coat tight around me and stride through a side door. I've been to the hospital so many times in the last two months that everything now is familiar. I glide through the back hallways, avoid the main elevators where people often carry candy, cards, and balloons, and get off on the fourth floor. The heels of my shoes make a click, click, clicking sound as I approach Sam's room. One of the nurses at the big oval desk, a young woman named Stephanie, smiles and greets me. "He's resting," she says. "Mrs. Nicholson is with him."

"Rest is about all he can do now, I suppose," I say to her.

"Yes. Not much else. We all love rest, but not when rest is the only option."

Outside of Sam's room, I pause and tilt my head close to the small opening of the door, listening, not wanting to intrude on a sublime moment. No sound comes from the room. I look back at Stephanie, who nods to tell me it is okay to enter. I quickly push through the door, quietly, into the dim light. On the other side of the room, I see Ruth.

"Hello, Marcus. Thank you."

She smiles, but it is a weary smile and her body seems to droop. Ruth, oh, Ruth, you were always the vibrant one, the one who led games of kick the can in the neighborhood until the last child was called home on those summer evenings, the one who jogged five mornings a week before the sun rose, the one we thought would never grow old. But at this moment, you too seem to have aged. I'm sorry, Ruth, so very sorry, that time has passed a craggy hand over you.

"How is he?" It's all I can think of to say, and it is a silly question to ask the wife of a dying man.

"Not much change. He's never really awakened today. The doctor came by this morning, but he didn't say much. They have him so medicated. I hope he isn't in horrid pain. I know what is happening, and that is all I wish for him, that it is not too painful."

"I'm sure he isn't in too much pain," I say, with more conviction than I really feel.

She looks at Sam, then back at me, and I know that I will need to listen well and say something wise. It is a small concession age brings, that wisdom comes more easily when you are old. "It's time, isn't it, Marcus? Time for a passage; time for a release. I fought it for so long, but now I know. Is it wrong for me to say that? Should I cling to him every moment? I feel confused much of the time now."

"It's okay, Ruth. Yes, it is time. It is all about enduring right now, I suppose. Don't feel lessened because of thoughts like those. It is time, and I think you know it, and I know it, and Sam knows it. I imagine him at a bridge, waiting to cross, his head turning slowly away from us."

She bends quickly and picks up her coat and purse.

4

"There's a cheese sandwich. I got it from the machine this afternoon, but I wasn't really hungry and couldn't eat it. If you get hungry, here it is. You can have it." She puts on her coat, and I help her with the sleeves. "You will call me if there is any change in the slightest? Any at all. Please."

"Yes, I will call. You need some rest. If you can close your eyes and just not move, you'll feel better. I will watch him as much as I can. I took a nap this afternoon, and I feel like a lion right now."

She moves toward the door. "You a lion, Marcus? A gentle lion, maybe." She looks back at the hospital bed and stares at her husband of forty-eight years. "At the bridge," she murmurs. "Wise Marcus says you're at a bridge. All too fast, my sweet Sam."

The door clicks behind her.

I pull up a chair next to the cot the hospital has provided. I look at my friend Sam for a few moments. His eyes are closed, and his hair, now patchy, is more white and less silver than a few short months ago. He breathes, but barely, lightly, his chest almost imperceptibly lifting and falling.

I talk to my old friend, which is a good feeling for the elderly, much better than discounted hamburgers and parking places one space removed from the handicapped spaces.

"Well, here we are, Brother Nicholson. Who called this meeting anyway? A couple of old high priests like us, with all this time and no meetings to go to. We used to look at all those old men when we were younger, those men with lines on their faces who slept on warm Sunday afternoons during sacrament meeting. We never thought we'd be like them; we thought we'd always be young and then be changed in the twinkling of an eye. But it happened to us, didn't it? Now we're old high priests too. We joked about it for so many years. Now look what has become of us."

I pause, feeling slightly childish talking to my slumbering friend.

"I'll take care of you this night, Sam. Stay with us. Ruth needs a few winks. Can you hold on until she gets back in the morning? I know you'd do anything for her. If I happen to doze and maybe dream, don't do anything rash. I could never look straight into Ruth's eyes again. Hang on a little longer, friend. The kids will be here by tomorrow evening. Hang on, Sam. When you say good-bye, let Ruth be at your side."

Stephanie opens the door and peers in. "Everything okay?"

"Yes, everything is fine," I say, hoping she didn't hear me speaking to Sam.

I look at him again.

"We have a long night ahead of us."

I reach over and put my hand on his forehead. I pull the blanket closer to him. I pat his hand and slump back in the chair and begin to watch the clock as the seconds, then the minutes, and later the hours of a good life continue to slip away.

CHAPTER TWO

August, blistering August, a sun so harsh that it pales even the summer sky. A fine haze of dust and grit drape our city. All is listless and simmering and shimmering. In 1957 air-conditioning is still an infant and a novelty, so we find refuge in shade and breezes and by sprinkling our roofs with water and from big, noisy fans on the tops of our houses, until the sun dips behind the hills to the west and brings temporary relief. These are good days for stillness and shadows and tall glasses of water and ice cubes waiting nearby. Helen reports that our two daughters, Kate and Debra, guzzled two pitchers of Kool-Aid this afternoon alone.

All of this heat and haze, these days of sapped strength and of discomfort, and the beans are in.

"You should go," says Helen on the sweltering Friday night. "They need help at the cannery. A Brother Nicholson says so. The beans will go to waste."

If Mormons keep the Sabbath day holy, it is only with the allowance that they keep Friday night and most of Saturdays sacred for other things. "I do not want to go to the cannery. I'm tired," I protest.

"I hate to see food wasted. Beans, especially. Someone needs them."

"I wanted time to myself tonight. I wanted time with you."

She cuts through my ill-conceived defense with one

swift, sure stroke. "You wanted time to read a magazine. You wanted to sit in the bathtub for an hour. You would have watched TV, and if I'm lucky you would have sat by me then and maybe patted my hand. Those beans will be wasted. You have your duty." She stops, then adds the cruelest of blows. "You have the priesthood," she says.

We priesthood holders have our duties, I acknowledge. We have the cannery and building projects and home teaching and most of the long meetings, and occasionally we must sit in judgment.

"You don't know anyone here yet. We've been here only two weeks. You can go to the cannery tonight and make some new friends. It will be good for you."

This sounds vaguely similar to what my mother would say when it was the first day of school and I was in the second grade and decided I had a stomachache and didn't want to go. It's true: I really want to stay at my home tonight and read my magazine and dangle my feet in water and maybe hold my wife's hand. I know I have made certain covenants that pretty much mean I should drop whatever I am doing and get on with building the kingdom, even if the kingdom on this particular night is made of beans. I know that I'm not being called out of my chair at general conference and sent on a mission for five years and leaving my wife and our children and our farm. But the fact remains that I don't want to go to the cannery and do beans tonight.

"You hold the priesthood," my wife reminds me again.

Since my stomach does not ache, the only honorable thing to do is go to the cannery. It is becoming painfully clear that what the Church has planned for me and what I have planned for me are two entirely different things. I wave a white flag.

"I will go to the cannery. It will not be fun. I will come

home cranky, tired, and not at all interesting, and I will smell like string beans. If you accept these conditions, I will go."

"Lawyers. I married a lawyer," she says before walking to the back door and calling in our daughters as they pour the last of the Kool-Aid over their heads. "You always put conditions on things. If they have a good buy on the beans, pick some up."

Less than an hour later, I am in the cannery, sitting on a mountain of steamy canned beans.

Someone needs to sit on the top of the heap and count the cans and stack them as they come out of the labeling machine. The shift manager took one look at my long, lean frame and asked me if I could catch cans of beans. I said yes, and he directed me to the top of the bean-can mountain, where the radiating heat tops the outdoor temperature by ten degrees or more.

I have decided the Lord put Church canneries on the earth to help the poor and needy and to keep a good many of the rest of us humble. It is hard to feel that you are special and part of a royal generation when you are sitting on thousands of cans of beans and the temperature is 110 degrees and it is a Friday night and your wife is at home playing with your children.

Perhaps the other reason for Church canneries is to bring forth talents that even you did not realize you had. For on this steamy, sweaty, miserable night, I am finding that I can catch bean cans with the best of them. The cans fly up, nice, soft lobs. My pitcher is a man of average size and build, about my age, but with silver prematurely weaving through his hair. He smiles and occasionally asks me how I am doing, and I always tell him, "Fine," although I'm not sure that is the case. He and I find a rhythm. Grab, toss, catch, stack. Grab, toss, catch, stack.

"One hundred!" I shout, as I have been instructed to do when another century of bean cans is stacked. Sweat streams down my face, but I am finding a strange sort of pleasure in making the mountain grow. Grab, toss, catch, stack. "One hundred!" Grab, toss, catch, stack.

For no good reason other than his ability to gently launch cans of beans my way, I begin to admire my battery mate. Grab, toss, catch, stack. An hour goes by, then two. The beans will not go to waste on my watch. At ten o'clock, the last of the beans has been canned and I slowly climb off the bean mountain. My bean-tossing counterpart is awaiting me.

"We're a good pair," he says, extending his hand. "Born for beans."

"A new career awaits us," I say, reaching out my hand.

"My name is Sam Nicholson. I think we're in the same ward."

"I'm Marcus Hathaway. I am new to the ward."

"Let me guess. You are an accountant."

"No. I'm an attorney."

He looks surprised. "I would have bet you were an accountant because you are an extraordinarily good bean counter."

And for the first of many times in my life, Sam Nicholson causes me to laugh.

We walk out of the cannery and into the night, which now seems softer and cooler.

Soon I am at home, where the lights are out and the high-pitched whirring of the fan is the only sound. I check our girls, then quietly get cleaned up before lying down in bed.

"Are you tired and cranky?" Helen asks sleepily. I had not known she was awake.

"Yes, I am tired and cranky, and the work was hard,

and please do not ask me to do much tomorrow. I stacked cans of beans by the thousands, and my back hurts, and I lost five pounds. I am a more humble man, however, than the one who left our home three hours ago."

"Then all was not lost. You learned something."

"I did. And I might have made a new friend. You were right about that, although I felt like a second grader when you said that to me."

She rolls over and kisses me and then turns away.

"I'm always right," she says contentedly, just before sleep whisks me away.

My dreams that night are of cool, long waterfalls cascading over a precipice of canned green beans.

* * *

Night wraps itself around our city. I stand and look outside the hospital window. Lights, amber in color, mark the edges of the parking lot and line the drive that leads from the hospital. Farther, toward the center of town, white, red, and yellow lights twinkle and flash, beckoning and illuminating. Inside, a single tube of light shines efficiently over the head of Sam's bed. Almost two hours have passed since Ruth left. Once, Sam moans in his sleep; another time his arm twitches. I look at him again. His face seems more hollow, his breathing more labored. Should I call Stephanie? Are these changes notable enough to notify Ruth?

"Remember our contract, Sam. Nothing tonight. No dramatic changes. Ruth would be disappointed in me and devastated by you, and she is yours for eternity and it might take that long before she would forgive you for leaving unannounced. No bad behavior tonight, my friend."

I return to the large, comfortable chair. Almost in answer to my concern, Stephanie carefully opens the door.

"How are we doing?"

"The same, I think. He seems to be having a difficult time breathing, but I can't really say if he has changed. I wonder if we should call his wife."

She comes close to his bed. She looks at him carefully, listens for a moment. "No. I don't think so. We're not quite ready for that."

It is odd, I think. I am twice and more the age of Stephanie. Yet she knows more about what to look for at times such as these. She is cheerful and competent, and I am glad for her brief company and professional judgment this night. I am glad that she is youthful in a room with two old men. Age has taught me that, one by one, you must eventually relinquish duties and judgments to younger people, even the care of yourself and perhaps of your spouse. While giving away what you do and a little of what you are is not always pleasant, it is better done gracefully and without resistance, I think.

"Call me if you have any questions. I'm on until eleven. I don't know if Dr. Flanders will be by tonight. You'd better get something to eat too. I don't want you in here next, Marcus." She smiles and wags her finger at me and turns to leave the room.

The phone rings. It is Ruth.

"Any changes?"

"No. The nurse was just here, and she said everything is about the same."

"I can't sleep, Marcus. I tried. I really tried. Do you ever get so tired that you can't sleep?"

"Yes, I've been that way a few times. Not many."

"What shall I do?"

"Call Helen. Talk with her. Watch an old movie. Read a book. Eat chocolate ice cream. Then be still in a dark, comfortable place, and sleep will come. You need only a few hours of rest. Maybe just doze a little. It will come, and Sam and I will get along just fine tonight, and you need not worry about how things are at the hospital."

She sighs. I know all of my good male advice to her doesn't mean much. She will be anxious, she will think of nothing but her Sam, and her mind will flood with pictures of days gone by. Sleep will come, but it will not come easily for her this night.

"Are you going to be okay?" I ask.

"Yes, I will be okay. It hasn't been easy and I know the worst is yet to come, but I will be okay, Marcus."

"Try to rest now."

She hangs up, and I know she will not do a single thing I have recommended.

"That's quite a girl you have there, Sam. I wouldn't be in a hurry to leave either."

And for the first time in the evening, Sam stirs and says something that, while I can't quite make out the words, I think I understand.

CHAPTER THREE

"I feel stupid, Sam. What is the point of all this?"

"You are thinking like the lawyer you are. Or an engineer or a mathematician. You need some loosening up, Marcus. You're wound too tight. You think that perfect justice must be accomplished in this world and that you alone are responsible for it. Relax. Now, remember the Vs should point right up your shoulder. Close your stance a bit. You don't have to hit it hard to make it go far. Good grief. I think it's easier to teach this game to an idiot than it is to a man with a college degree. Doubly hard for a University of Chicago law school graduate."

I stare at a dimpled, white golf ball, sitting on a tee, tantalizingly close.

"You don't understand, Marcus. There is something primal and very satisfying about knocking the daylights out of it. I don't know what they did when they lived in caves and didn't have golf to help them work out life's frustrations."

"They used their clubs to kill woolly mammoths and saber-toothed tigers that would otherwise stomp them or eat them. That's how they took out their frustrations," I say petulantly.

"This will be good for you. Now stop waggling your club. It will be satisfying for you to hit the ball."

"I suppose. But it seems a good way to spoil an otherwise fine day."

And a fine day it was, early spring, no clouds to be seen. The day promised gauzy, good warmth, a day of buds transfigured to blossoms, a day when the very cellar of the earth, sealed tight since late October, would open and speak words of refreshment and revival to all who walked upon it. The first good day of spring it was, and I was standing on a golf course, a three wood in hand, looking down a velvet-green fairway toward a slim, white pole with a narrow, red flag hanging from it.

This is one of those things that I have never heard from the pulpit, and I don't know if even Brigham Young said it, although he said almost everything at least once, but I think each day is alive and has its own character and that when people say, "Oh, I had a good day," or "My day was terrible," there really might be more to it than just how we chose to fill it. I once told Helen of this belief of mine, and she shook her head and said sometimes I see things that aren't really there, but nevertheless I believe this about days. If I am right, this particular day's character was kind and gentle, and I was spending the first three hours of it on a golf course, and more than that, I had paid five dollars for the privilege of trying to whack a little, dimpled ball into a small hole many yards away.

"Well, it is stupid," I repeated to Sam.

He stopped his instruction for a moment and looked at me. I thought he would say, *Well, if you feel that strongly about it, we can just go home and enjoy the remainder of the morning, and I'll never take you golfing again.*

But he did not say that. Instead he said, "Marcus, you know I am a religious man, and golf is part of what I believe in. You need to show more faith. You will like this game, and someday you will thank me and praise my name for having introduced it to you. Now hit the ball, and stop making excuses and thinking too much about things."

I looked around. Most of the men wore funny, loud clothes, and I'd noticed some caps that made me think that these were middle-aged or older people trying to look young. I liked it when I heard, muffled and soft, someone say, "Straight and true. Nice shot, Robert," and I liked the funny expressions I heard, such as "Stiff on the stick, Willie boy," or "Grab it, grab it, grab it, Mr. Green," or "Holy jumping up and down Aunt Tilly, what a putt."

"You'll hear words that will make you wince, but it is part of golf," Sam had warned me earlier, and he was right. The sky was blue that day, and the air was sometimes blue too.

"I am happy here, with my golf ball close to me," I said to Sam when we were ready to tee off on the first hole. "I don't want the golf ball to go away. It is new and shining and perfect, and if I hit it the ball will only become dirty and scarred or perhaps end up lost in the tall grass or in a lake. The golf ball is my friend. I do not want to send it away. Golf must not be like life, where you keep things important close to you and you don't push them away," I said.

"It is more like life than you think, Marcus. You cannot keep very many things close to you for very long, and you're old enough to know that. And you are trying to intellectualize the game, which cannot be done. Never again call a golf ball your friend. You can be a thinker on the golf course and you can be a philosopher, but you cannot be an intellectual, so stand up there and try to smack the ball into the next county. It will feel good when you do."

I saw a sand trap on the left, far down the fairway, and it looked so inviting with its creamy-brown ripples. On the next fairway over, a sprinkler hissed and clapped rhythmically, shooting a fine sheen of water behind the green. The golf course, I conceded, was lovely, and maybe the money

I paid was worth the walk in such a pleasant place. Perhaps I could just walk around the course as Sam played.

"Go ahead and hit it," Sam urged. "Keep your right elbow tucked in more toward your rib cage, or you will slice your drive, which means it will take a giant arc to the right and make it more difficult to get where you want to be. And keep your head down. Always keep your head down. Can't steal a peek at all, Marcus. The golf ball is very unforgiving of those who are caught looking at it at the wrong time. Almost as unforgiving as when Lot's wife looked back."

Reluctantly, I locked my gaze on the golf ball. I wiggled my hips and waggled my club a little because I had seen professional golfers do that on television. I stared at the ball and vowed to keep my eye on it, no matter what.

I started the club back slowly, a great, wide, tedious arc, brought it to a halt, cocked my hips, and then moved them forward. Something came over me, and it felt good and sweet as my club head came through the swing. My hips exploded, the club made a sumptuous click, and I felt pleased and happy and satisfied and accomplished all at once.

Golf, I have since concluded, is at its best when it makes you feel that way, which it doesn't as often as I wish it would.

When I did look up, I saw the ball flying away on a low line. Like an airplane that reaches the right speed to lift up, the ball gracefully rose in the air. I thought I heard a shearing sound as it split through the dewy morning air. The ball plopped pleasantly in the middle of the wide greenway, bounced impishly three times, and rolled another twenty yards.

I stood, transfixed, a good day now becoming something more beautiful and intricate.

Sam said nothing.

"That was nice," I murmured.

I was hooked on golf.

We played together for almost forty years, in the summer, two or three times a week sometimes. Even in the winter, we put on our clumsy rain gear and tromped around the courses. Only snow stopped us, although once we showed up when there was a half-inch of white on the ground, a can of orange spray paint in Sam's hand, a look of longing on our faces, and we painted a half-dozen golf balls and tried our luck.

We would become good at this game. Sam's game was short and precise, calculating, shaving off a stroke here and there, always at or around the green. My game was long. In the days before technology took over the game, in the days before exotic metal clubs and golf balls wound so tight they almost jumped off the tee, I could knock a ball 265 yards.

Our last game of golf together was two Octobers before, when most of the leaves had dropped and the grass of the fairway was brown and sad and the character of the day seemed to say, *I am tired, and I want to be finished, and I don't feel beautiful at all.*

Sam carded an 89.

* * *

Outside in the hallway, I hear the noise of someone looking at Sam's chart. I expect a doctor momentarily. Sam is again very still in the dim light of the hospital room.

The doctor's visit is brief, which is what you expect when it is too much even to pray for a miracle, when all you really want is a quiet passage with as little pain as possible, because your hope is gone, locked away in a dark cellar somewhere. This is the time when enduring to the end becomes real and not a concept that you read about in the scriptures or hear intoned over the pulpit. Most times, enduring is not very much fun and more difficult than it sounds, and we're usually asked to endure most just when we want things to be quick or pleasant or both.

"If he changes at all, let the nurse know," Dr. Flanders says. "You might see him take on a kind of gray coloration, and if that happens, call, although I think he may be a few days away from it." The doctor turns his slim, slumped shoulders and walks from the room.

I look at Sam and then turn to look out the window, where the lights sparkle and cars zoom by on the highway, and thousands of people hurry on their way home. I feel envious of them and long for the time when I can join their numbers and not have to stand by and watch as an old and true friend dies.

The ledge in Sam's room is brimming with cards bearing messages that are sad, stately, sappy, or funny. I know that Sam would like the funny ones best. I pick up one of the cards that looks funny and am startled when a photograph slips out. The photo is an old one, the colors washed out. Six youthful faces stare from the photo, with an adult, Sam, standing by them. I turn the photo over in my hand and read words scrawled on the back: *Canopy Lake, 1959. You were the best Scoutmaster ever.*

The words are not hyperbole. I had gone on enough campouts with Sam to know differently. Sam was a great Scoutmaster, and it pleases me that one of his boys has taken the time so many years later to acknowledge that. When a man lies dying, one of the best tributes he can receive is to say that he was a good Scoutmaster.

I take a step to the big chair in the corner of the room. The picture is still in my right hand. I hold it up in the scarce light and say the names out loud: Arthur Wilson.

Ben Simmons. Howard Blake. John Parsons. Phillip Anderson. And Rob Nicholson, Sam's own son. They all stand there grinning, fish in the scarce grass in front of them, trophies from their overnight adventure. Sam stands on their right, his funny, old fishing hat shading his features. I scour the photo again. Am I the one who took it? I think so. Would it be the campout when John Parsons caught his first fish?

I close my eyes. I dream, though I do not sleep.

The creek rushes by, stony in places, its waters swift, then slow, then swift again. It empties from the lake, and I watch it, thinking these drops will end up as an ocean. Canopy Lake sits in a bowl carved from granite on the left shoulder of a towering ridgeline. It is August, and there are still pockets of snow within a ten-minute hike over the boulders. The lake is high in the mountains, and there is no canopy of trees, only stubby grasses and wild mint under the thin, scattered straight pines. I wonder about the lake's name until I lie down at night and look heavenward and see a million stars, clear, bright, radiant, and flickering, and understand that the sky is the canopy and at once feel so small that I could be a speck of dust and so large that I know all of this was created by a God who loves me and loves the mountains too.

And when the canopy fades in the morning and sunlight swathes our lake in gold, we have a mission as a troop: John Parsons has never caught a fish, a fact well known among the boys, and it is something in his life that must be corrected soon.

John is tall, red-haired, well liked, and even now, when I see blazing stars in a milky canopy overhead, I often think of him.

"Enough is enough," Sam says to the group on Friday night. "Tomorrow John catches a fish. I guarantee that will be the case. In the morning, before daylight, I will sit in my chair and think for a bit, but by sunrise, I expect all of you up, rods in hand, and together we will watch John catch his fish."

Morale in the camp shoots skyward, almost touching the tips of the stars. John looks pleased, the yellow flame of our campfire reflecting fiercely in his eyes. His drought will end tomorrow because Brother Nicholson has said so. Somewhere in the dark water nearby rests a fish that will be John's tomorrow.

We grow cold overnight at that high elevation and hardly sleep.

First light. Voices, excited. Gentle encouragement. "C'mon John, get up. Brother Nicholson is already in his chair waiting."

The sun peeps over the ridge, splashing Canopy Lake in a cold, red hue. We are walking to the creek, where water that was snow only two weeks before spins, churns, and plunges away from the lake toward the Pacific like a child tearing away from his mother. The fishing would be good here in the dark, deep hole downstream from where the lake bleeds into the creek.

"John. Come here," Sam commands. The other boys fan out downstream or close to the edge of the lake. "I have my rod all rigged. Let me trade mine for yours."

He takes Sam's rod gingerly. It is a very good rod, and Sam is a very good fisherman. John is respectful, as though Willie Mays has just asked him to put on his glove while they play catch. I think, *John is a good young man. He understands the situation. Maybe I will let him date my eldest daughter in a few more years.*

The sun rises higher, driving the chilliness from inside me. Its rays slant into the river canyon, knifing through the early-morning shadows. I back away from Sam and John and fiddle with my own gear. *Please let this work*, I think. *Sam, I hope you are right. John needs a fish.*

"The sun is just about right. If you drop the fly into the deep water on the other side of the current, you will get a fish," Sam whispers. "Just behind that big rock, in the slack water. That's where they are. I can think like a fish, and that's where they are, I know it."

John perches on a rock near the stream.

"Your fly should be light on the water. Like a bug. Bugs don't splash or slap, they alight on the water. A fish is in there, John."

Sam fishes only with flies. He thinks those who fish with bait are like the uncircumcised. He thinks that no one who holds the Melchizedek Priesthood should be allowed to fish with bait. He thinks it is a telestial way to fish.

And after giving this subject considerable thought for almost forty years, I agree with him, although I do not expect it will be part of the temple recommend questions in my lifetime.

John studies the water intently and takes a deep breath. He cocks his arm, as Sam coaches gently, "Not too far back. Pull up. Remember, the fly must *alight*."

The morning sun breaks on John as he stands on his rock. His line shines in the lightness. His face is a study in concentration, and his teeth dig hard into his lower lip. The line whips forward, whips backward, following the fabled ten o'clock, two o'clock motion. The other boys stop fishing. All eyes are on John. Sunlight dances off the water like a million little sparkles. I hope and pray that Sam is right, that there is a fish waiting for breakfast in a dark stream hole, and that the fish will be silly enough to mistake a small bundle of feathers and fine twine for a morning meal.

The moment is finely scratched in memory. The fly

delicately drops, and Sam mouths the words, "Perfect, John. Perfect." The fly sits on the water daintily, its dark mission hidden, a bit of cork shank and feathers floating idly on waters that will roil in the sea weeks from now. A slight movement comes from just below the surface, and a fish breaks water. My heart stops, leaps, then beats furiously. The line jerks taut. John yelps, and Sam shouts, "Play your line! He'll go deep on you! Give him some slack, and when he stops running, pull the line in! He's yours, John, he's yours!"

A fat, shimmering rainbow trout thrashes to the surface, then drops deep again. John lets the line loosen, then pulls it in. It is not a perfect landing, but somehow John manages to get the fish ashore, where it flips and flops and spins, the dance of death beginning.

"First cast, John. I've never done that," Sam says, which I think is not true, but since it is a lie to build a boy, I am sure it is forgiven as soon as it is spoken.

John beams. The other deacons laugh and whoop, and no matter what else happens that day, it is beautiful and Sam's legend as a Scoutmaster grows. Years later, a new generation of deacons and Scouts arises, long after Sam's release as Scoutmaster, and I hear the talk in the hallways at church. "Brother Nicholson is the best. He knows where the fish are. He thinks like a fish."

I open my eyes. I look again at the photo of twelve-year-old and thirteen-year-old boys, skinny and freckled, not knowing who they are. Life is a puzzle to them, although they are learning a few answers. So innocent, those concoctions of croaking voices, fuzzy cheeks, and boundless energy, stumbling over objects real and imagined, trying to stand on slippery rocks as waves roll shoreward.

I think I'd rather be seventy-one than thirteen.

But they were good fellows, even then. Arthur. Ben. Howard. Phillip. Rob.

And John.

My heavens, sweet, beautiful John, his red hair catching the sunbeams on the banks of Canopy Creek, holding a fourteen-inch fish as though it were gold.

Regal. He seemed so regal at that moment on a shore of a lake on a summer morning.

Yes, they were good fellows even then, and they had the best Scoutmaster in the world.

Eight years later, John sat in a helicopter in a burned area near green jungle, opened the door, and tried to help in the wounded. He never had a chance. He didn't hurt very long.

And at his funeral, someone mentioned the Saturday morning at Canopy Lake and John's first fish ever. We were casket bearers, Sam and I, and Sam's shoulders heaved and his hands trembled when the speaker told the story, but his eyes never moved, and it was only later that evening that he sobbed like a baby for his Scout John.

He went to the Parsons's home that night and handed a very fine fishing rod to Brother and Sister Parsons. "It's really John's. Ever since he caught that trout, this rod has been his more than mine." And we all cried again.

"I told John the fish was his, but that is not true," Sam said on our way home. "The fish wasn't John's, and John really wasn't Bill and Frances's. I know it doesn't make sense, but I feel that. Sometimes what you feel is more true than what you think. Do you understand?"

I said, "I understand, and it is a hard thing to learn."

Canopy Lake remains beautiful, but Sam and I visited it only one more time together after John's death. Sam didn't fish that time, but at first light, when he thought I was asleep, I saw him go to a spot where the dark water ran like a black highway into a canyon with no end. He had a few mountain wildflowers and some mint in his hand, and he tossed them lightly—made them *alight*, if you will—on the water.

My eyes open, my dream turned dark. I walk over to the bed and hold the photo before Sam's closed eyes. "When you get there, Sam, please say hello to John Parsons for me. He was really a fine fellow, you know."

CHAPTER FOUR

I am restless and feeling faded. I look at my watch, and it is not quite ten o'clock. A television set is on the wall, and I think for a moment that I should turn it on and let it provide me with companionship, which is something you value more as you grow old. But something doesn't seem right about watching television with my friend dying at my side. I don't watch television very much, just an old mystery now and then and sometimes a show about wildlife on public television. That's about it. I don't even sneak to the far room in our home on Sunday afternoons to watch football any more.

What I need is affirmation, what I need is revival, what I need is life. This is a hospital, after all, where some people come and never leave but where some arrive for the first time. I wander outside Sam's room and past the nurses' station. At the end of the hallway I take the stairway down one flight and turn to my right, where there is a long wall, windowed, with two panes of angled glass meeting in the middle, which for some reason reminds me of the bow of a ship. Beyond the walls are babies, new babies, some only hours old. This is where I will reaffirm life.

On one side of the oblique glass are little, red, wrinkly babies with blue caps and splotchy skin. On the other side, where the glass juts outward, are little, red, wrinkly babies with pink caps and splotchy skin.

I look at them. Most of them are quiet except for a

little girl on the far right of the window, and she is the one I immediately like best. I cannot see the cards at the heads of the little, plastic bassinets, so I do not know her name. "You will be Harold," I say to her. Harold squawks and squawks, and nobody seems to hear. "It will get worse, Harold. And it will get better. You are one or two days old, and I know landings in this life are rough, and you have every right to be upset because you came from a better place. Count this as your first experience. It will be one of many, and you will learn from most of them if you are wise, Harold. I am pleased to make your acquaintance."

I am giving a fine speech to Harold, I think, but she still doesn't seem to like this part of her earthly experience.

"I am glad that our paths crossed. I wish you a long and healthy life, a family who loves you. I hope you will be a mom someday and that you will be shielded from sadness, except in small doses, which I suppose we all need to experience so that we can grow. I hope you have a pretty, new dress to wear on your first day of school. I hope your mother has many bright hair bows for you. I hope that you will find something good and exciting in each day and that you are never left alone at the playground while all the other girls play jump rope.

"I am sorry that you missed my friend Sam, although you came close to one another. There was a chance that you could have met him as he came up and you came down, but the timing wasn't right. At least you shared some time together in this place. You would have liked Sam, and he would have liked you, Harold."

To my surprise and pleasure, Harold stops crying and her eyelids sag. Soon she is asleep.

This is a small miracle to me. I think I see more miracles now than when I was younger, and watching a baby fall asleep is still akin to a miracle, in my view.

A nurse comes in on the other side of the big, glass window and checks all the babies. I envy her, always being around newness, noise, and wonder. Harold raises a sleepy eyelid of acknowledgment, then rests sweetly.

Babies, I think, are beautiful.

The nurse looks at me and smiles. I raise my hand and wave to her. And my mind wanders again toward Sam, babies, friends, and a time that seemed more simple than now.

* * *

It is winter, dark and cold. Helen is expecting our third child. On a day when the big, electric clock next to our bed shows it is not yet three in the morning, I feel Helen stir.

"Are you okay?"

"I don't know. Marcus, I think my water just broke."

"Oh. Is that good?"

Across the dark bed, I can almost feel her response. *Men*.

Then I feel squishy sheets. I bolt upright in bed, then dive over Helen's considerable mass and land on the other side of our bed. "What on earth?"

"Our electric blanket is on. I want it off. I do not want to be electrocuted. It wouldn't look good in the headlines. 'Couple Die in Bed When Pregnant Wife's Water Breaks.' We'd be talked about on Jack Paar's show. I would rather go in a car wreck."

I sense the one word again, from the miles that separate me on the floor from her on the bed. *Men*. And as an afterthought, *I had to go and marry one*.

"Do we wait until morning?"

Helen sits up in bed with great effort. "No. We go to the hospital. And we wouldn't have been electrocuted. Marcus, you've been here before. When the water breaks, the baby is coming. This is our third, and the last one came quickly, so this one will probably be even faster."

"But you aren't due for another three weeks."

"Tell that to our daughter. She sets the rules."

"Daughter? I would like a son this time, please."

"She is a daughter. And you will love her more than any other baby in the world."

"What about Kate and Debra?"

"We need to call someone. Mother isn't coming for two weeks."

I think of Sam and the beans in the cannery on a hot Friday night, and a slight feeling that I will call vengeance tingles within me, proving that getting even can sometimes be considered a spiritual experience.

"I'll call Sam Nicholson."

"He is a schoolteacher. He needs to get up in a couple of hours and teach school all day."

"I'll call him anyway."

"Please, just solve it. At this stage, it feels like an earthquake is taking place inside me, and if we talk about this much longer I will deliver the baby right here, and we don't want that to happen. Go now, Marcus. Call someone."

Sam's voice was groggy, as expected. "Yes, sure, I'll come right over. Be right there. Don't worry about school. I can find a sub, or Ruth can come over."

Ten minutes later, as we pack the last of Helen's things, Sam is at our door. He has on a pair of wrinkled slacks and a sweatshirt, and his hair is tousled, and he has big, round, blue circles under his eyes.

"Top of the mornin'," he greets us. "It's a fine day for having a baby, isn't it, Mrs. Hathaway?"

Helen eyes both of us with something akin to contempt, and I can again feel her one-word, one-syllable, one-emotion response: *Men*.

But she softens, perhaps because she knows what is ahead and that she can't hold a grudge forever. "Honey, we need to go. This isn't getting any easier."

We bustle out the door. "Good luck, Helen," Sam says. "Don't worry about your girls. We will care for them."

We drive to the hospital through dark streets and a night with long, icy fingers. Because times were different then, my wife is ushered in and I am instructed to take my place in the waiting room.

Now, much is made about men holding the priesthood and women getting to be wives and mothers, and we men sometimes put on long faces about how heavily laden we are with the awesome and perpetual responsibility that the priesthood brings and how we have many important matters to deal with and how it calls for us to attend many meetings and to counsel and deliberate with great solemnity and also to attend father-and-son campouts.

I know it is true that the priesthood does mean we have lots of responsibilities, and I have a hunch we are getting only a brief glimpse of them here on earth, but I have yet to meet one priesthood holder who has said, "I'd rather have a baby." Going to the hospital for the birth of our third child brought it all back to me about why men really do have the easier end of the whole deal.

So it is not without some relief that I slink into the waiting room with two or three other fathers, all of us instantly bound by a moment and an event at once unique and at once shared. I sit down and try to look nonchalant and think myself mildly successful at accomplishing this, although I study my magazine page for twenty minutes and still can't remember the topic of the article.

Our first babies came rather quickly, but this one is different. The sun rises, the day takes its form and shape, and there is no baby. A nurse occasionally comes out and updates one of the other fathers in the room, but not much is said to me. Finally the nurse comes into the room and says, "Mr. Hathaway?"

"That's me," I answer.

"You may go see your wife now. She is fine, but it appears the baby is breech, and we may need to perform a C-section on her."

I think I know the answer, but I ask anyway, "Is that serious?"

"Usually not. The doctor is here, and we'll make the decision later in the morning."

I look at my watch, and it is almost nine o'clock. I follow the nurse into a gleaming, bright, tiled room in which no germ would ever dare show up.

"Hello, honey. How are you doing?" I ask Helen.

Helen does not suffer fools when she is in labor. She gives me a look that fairly shouts, *Don't be dense, Marcus. I am in great pain. Childbirth is not fun for me. Imagine pulling your eyelids down to your knees, and you might begin to get the picture. The heck with dignity. I want to shout and scream and get this over with.* But she manages a glimmer of a smile and says, "I'm okay," and I think I love her more because of her answer.

The day slips by. I call home, and Ruth answers. She says the girls are fine and not to worry. Sam is at school, and she brought her youngest children to our home for the day, and they are all playing and will have soup and peanut butter sandwiches for lunch. She says, "Give our love to Helen. Everything is fine here, and you two don't need to worry."

So we get back to the work of having a baby. Soon it is afternoon, then late afternoon, and Helen is in great pain, and every time I ask about the C-section decision, they shrug and say, "Let's wait a little longer."

31

Then things seem to get even more serious, and Helen's forehead is matted with perspiration, and her eyes are dark and filled with tears, and her mouth is a small, thin line. I know I should go because soon she will start saying rude things to me which I know she doesn't really mean, but they will come out of her mouth anyway, and I always remember them. The nurse understands that we are at a critical point and that the health of the mother, baby, and father, as well as the entire marriage, might soon be in peril. She banishes me to the waiting room, and it is a whole new crop of fathers that awaits me there, and I feel a new kind of responsibility because I am the senior father in the room.

I stop as they all eye me, and I say, "Everything's okay, guys," then they go back to their reading, milling, pacing, and watching TV.

I sit down, then I pace, then I sit down, then I try to read, but nothing works because nearby is the woman I love more than anyone else, and she is in great pain, and soon we will have a new baby and our lives will never be in the same orbit again. My thoughts, my feelings, my emotions are all a jumble, but I am the patriarch of the waiting room and feel that I should set an example for the younger fathers. I am worried, excited, struck with awe, and feeling helpless about everything that is around me. *Please*, I pray, *let everything be fine.*

Other fathers are called as their babies are born. A whole new generation springs up before my eyes. I begin to worry more and wonder how much longer all of this will go on.

Finally the door with the small, wire-crossed window opens. "Mr. Hathaway?" asks a representative of the third wave of nurses since we arrived this morning. I nod. "Come back with me, please."

"Is everything okay?"

"Yes, everything is okay," she reassures me.

I walk into a darkened room and let my eyes adjust. Around me is movement as the doctor and nurses finish their work. I see Helen, pale, exhausted, her hair wet and brown on her pillow, her eyes deep, and her breath short and shallow.

And on her breast is a little girl draped in a tiny, white gown, squinting, a shock of hair just like her mother's. And I look at her and say, "Hello." The baby girl becomes our Elizabeth Bryn Hathaway.

And Elizabeth is our last child because babies do not come easily to us, which also explains why there are a dozen years between our eldest and our youngest.

Now my eyes are moist, and I hold my infant daughter for the first time, and there is not a better feeling in this existence. "Thank you, Helen." It is all I can think of to say, and it will suffice.

I call home and tell Kate and Debra they have a new baby sister, and they yammer and shout their excitement. Sam, back on the night shift after Ruth, congratulates me. "A girl. Anyone can have a girl," he says, laughing.

I do not get home until midnight. When I walk in the house, I do so quietly. On the couch I see Kate sprawled out asleep, while Debra is curled into a rocking chair. On the floor, with a couch pillow under his head and an apron draped around his stomach, is Sam, sound asleep.

And I know at that moment, although I had thought it before, that Sam could be a friend for a lifetime and more, which should happen more often than it does. Why it does not I have yet to figure out, although I think it may have to do with people choosing things instead of relationships.

* * *

The tapping of footsteps brings me back from the day our Elizabeth was born in a hospital to the present, where my little friend Harold still sleeps. A woman who has given birth earlier in the day walks stiffly down the hallway, her hand against a wall, bracing herself.

"Good night, little Harold."

Elizabeth, my Betsy Bee. She is now past thirty and has never married, and we all wonder why some things have not worked out for her and if she will ever be a mother. She is a schoolteacher and talks about her students being her kids, but we think that is not the same. We see her sorrow and feel it and wish it would go away. I want to take away the lurking ache in her life because I am her father and it is never easy to see your children in pain.

"I don't feel pretty," she said to me three years ago at Thanksgiving. "I don't feel pretty at all," and her face was streaked with the curled trails of tears.

"You are beautiful, Elizabeth. You are beautiful, and do not think of yourself in any other way." That was all I could think of to say to her, and I still don't know if it was enough or right. I wish I were a wiser father.

I walk back to Sam's room, in my mind a picture of Harold sleeping in her little, pink cap. Tomorrow I will call Elizabeth, and I will meet her for lunch somewhere soon. We haven't talked much these last few weeks, and I need to hold her hands across the table and tell her once more that she is beautiful and that all will work out well.

It has been too long since I have done so.

In Sam's room, I sit down on the cot and turn my head toward the window and again stare into the night and the lights and think about how far away dawn seems to be. The door behind me opens, and I expect that it is Stephanie coming in to say good night.

"Marcus?"

It is my wife's voice.

"I didn't expect to see you here. It is getting close to eleven," I say.

"I couldn't sleep. I brought you some food. Not much. A turkey sandwich and applesauce and a carton of orange juice. How is he?"

"About the same. He has slept all the while I have been here."

Helen walks over to the bedside and holds Sam's hand. "Have you been at his side all night?"

"Most of the time. I walked to the nursery to see the new babies."

She looks up at me. "Made new friends?"

"Yes. Especially one. Her name is Harold."

"Harold? Someone named a baby girl Harold?"

"The someone who named her Harold is me."

Helen frowns, but there is no sense of disapproval.

"And I suppose you talked with her about life. Did you tell her about life's complexities and mysteries? Did you try to make her wise all at once?"

"I did. You know me well. But I talked with her only a little. I told her that I wanted her to be happy and not experience too much sadness and that I hoped people would care for her. That's all I told her. Harold is beautiful, as are all the other babies in the nursery."

Helen stands and walks toward me. It is dark enough in the room so that I cannot see her eyes, so I am unsure what she is thinking. Helen is tall and still has smooth skin. Her name before we married was Helen Renaldi, and she was one of the few people I had met of Italian ancestry who was a Church member. She has always had lovely skin, slightly dark, what most people would say is olive colored, although to me her skin looks nothing like the color of any olive I have ever seen. I think she is pretty, and at church not long ago I heard one of the Mia Maids say, "Sister Hathaway is so pretty. I want to look like her when I am older." It made me feel good to hear that, and I told Helen, and it made her feel good too. What she ever saw in me, I do not know. I am tall and thin and angular and was never very strong, but I guess she looked at me on the inside and thought I would be a good husband and father and honor my priesthood.

But now she is close, and I do not know what she will say. She looks at me for a second and then she speaks.

"You say the word *beautiful* a lot. Do you know that?"

"Yes, I know that. It is a very fine word. Once I thought perhaps I said it too much, but now I think I should say it more often."

"For forty years, you were an attorney, and you've seen people at their worst almost daily, and you still say *beautiful* more than any man I've ever known. I've envied you, Marcus, for seeing so much beauty, in places where not many of us can even bear to look."

And her words cause me to feel good and happy, even in the hospital room where my friend lies so ill.

"Thank you. And you, Helen, are also beautiful, in a different way than the little babies, but beautiful nonetheless." And I mean those words; I am not just saying them. As people grow older, their need to be told that they are beautiful and good and lovely and that their lives have meaning to others does not diminish. I think the need grows greater.

"Marcus," she says, and she steps close to me and kisses my forehead.

She steps back.

"Do you want to share the sandwich? I'm only a little hungry. I don't think Sam will mind if we eat in his presence," I say.

Helen smiles and says she will stay and share the little dinner with me. I break the sandwich in two, then find a cup and pour half of the juice in it. Helen insists I eat the applesauce myself. I sit on the window ledge, she sits in the chair, and together we eat, we talk, we remember, and for the second time in the evening, I discover something beautiful close by.

CHAPTER FIVE

Helen leaves a little after midnight. Sam's nurse, Stephanie, comes in and bids the two of us good night.

"I need to get on my way now. Have to stop at the grocery store. All out of milk, and the kids will need it for their cereal in the morning," she says. "There's a grocery store on the way home that stays open all night, so it's handy. I am one of the few people who enjoys grocery shopping at one in the morning. Crazy lives we lead, Marcus."

"Crazy indeed. We all hurry too much, and I think we miss more by going faster. Will I see you tomorrow?"

"If you're here. I work tomorrow and Saturday."

"Whether I'm here depends on whether Sam is here."

She blushes. "I'm sorry. I didn't mean it that way. He'll be here. That's my professional opinion. And personal feeling and hope." She stops and smiles mischievously. "And anytime you want to come home with me and be my children's grandfather, you only need to say so."

"I may surprise you sometime. Good night, Stephanie."

"Good night, Marcus."

She is kind, and it is calming to know that there is kindness among those who are so much younger. Most people her age look through or past people my age. We have so much more and are so much more than they think. But most of them will understand that fact only when they too become old.

Sam stirs slightly, and my hope rises for an instant that he will wake and recognize me. But he quickly quiets, and my thoughts flicker and start, stall, then settle again on sweet memories of kindnesses in other places and other times. I close my eyes and feel drowsy, and I hear music, slow and earnest, a musical bridge from thirty years before.

* * *

Five men in tuxedos stand on the stage and play the music of my dream. It is the night of our ward gold and green ball. Sam is the elders quorum president.

Brigham Young once said that Mormons, if left alone, are a fairly boring lot, and he was right, but the one exception might have been the ward gold and green ball, where both waltzes and stories swept through the cultural hall with magical aplomb. This night, our small cultural hall is bedecked in a way that I have never seen. Gold and green crepe paper hangs along the sides of the room. A fountain bubbles in the middle of the floor. Dozens of plants decorate the stage.

As president of the elders quorum, Sam is in and out of the kitchen all night, taking seriously the quorum's cleaning assignment, making frequent trips to the Dumpster in the parking lot. King Benjamin, who knew more than a little about serving with people, would have approved, I think.

"He's holding the trash more than he is holding you, Ruth," I say, and she shrugs her shoulders and replies, "Part of the calling, Marcus. I hope he came because of me and not because he is in charge of the trash."

The band plays not well but with earnestness, and since most members of our ward generally can't tell the difference between good music and not-good music, it makes little difference. This is a night of realization, of celebration, a time to be seen and if possible admired. We all imagine conversations that probably will not take place but that we enjoy thinking about anyway. "Didn't the Johnsons look nice tonight? Never would have pictured Earl in a tux." "Did you see how well the Mitchells danced? And he is so quiet. You never know. You never do." "And Brother Nilsson, the master of ceremonies. What a riot he was! He zinged Bishop Allred pretty well tonight, but he didn't mind. I think he laughed harder than almost anyone."

And so it goes, a time to see and a time to be seen. In their own way, gold and green balls were fun and interesting and happy occasions, and I wish they were still held.

"Time to go check the garbage," Sam says, the sound of duty trumpeting in his ears.

"No, I'll do it this time. I'm an elder too, and you need to delegate, even in such serious and sensitive matters as who will take out the garbage," I say, and Ruth gives me a quick wink of thanks.

I slip away from the knot of people and find my way to the kitchen. Inside I see some Relief Society sisters and a few of the high priests standing side-by-side washing dishes and putting more desserts on the serving cart. Some high priests would rather dry dishes than dance with their wives, which shows that wisdom is not necessarily a requisite of the ordination.

I also see Sister Callison scrubbing pots and pans while the music plays soft and simple and wholesome love songs, and the elders, who are much more expressive about such things than high priests, hold their wives close to them and dance slowly.

Sister Callison is divorced.

Divorce was so much more rare then and the stigma much harder to avoid. In Jenny Callison's case, she fell in love with a man named Scott, a returned missionary active in the Church, and he fell in love with her, helped teach her the missionary lessons, then baptized her and married her in the temple. And they should have lived happily ever after but did not.

The story is this: Her husband comes home one night after work and says that he is leaving her because he is in love with another woman he met at the office and that he never loved Jenny anyway, but he was young and mostly just felt sorry for her. He told her that he was bored and tired and needed a change and that there was no excitement in their relationship. Then he talked about his needs for this and that and his right to be happy and how he didn't feel fulfilled and how he owed it to himself to find contentment in his relationships, and said that he was leaving and that his lawyer would be in touch. "I hope you'll try to understand," he said as he left, and he didn't even kiss their two children good-bye. He packed a few things and drove away, and the lawyers took over.

And Jenny was so stunned that she couldn't talk, and it was only the following day that she began to cry, and she didn't stop for a week.

We worried about Jenny and her children. We worried that because she was still new in the Church and that because her husband left her while he carried a temple recommend in his pocket she might leave us.

We never should have worried, because she stayed strong and true.

And here she was, dressed in a lime-colored gown, her hair puffed up and combed over, wearing cream-colored shoes, a single woman, divorced, with the courage to come to a gold and green ball. Here she was, working away in the kitchen, while everyone else her age swept across the floor with their spouses, and Jenny Callison just scrubbed the casserole dishes harder and scraped the plates so clean they hardly needed to be washed, and she smiled and talked with the others in the kitchen crew, but a slight look of determination ringed her pretty features.

Jenny Callison came to work in the kitchen, but she also came hoping to dance.

And if Jenny Callison were a pioneer, not only would she have made it to the valley but she would have walked in front of the lead wagon.

I stared at her, and something inside me said I should do something, but I did not know what and worried about what other people might think. So I bundled up the trash and tried to not think of Jenny, because although I admired her, I felt awkward too.

I got outside of the kitchen and looked toward the cultural hall, and there was Sam whispering something to Ruth, who nodded, although she had an odd expression on her face. Sam walked by me and into the kitchen and approached Jenny Callison.

"Sister Callison, I would be greatly honored if you danced with me," I heard him say. You'd think the announcement had come from Salt Lake City that we were to pack up and march toward Missouri in the morning. Movement and chatter in the kitchen simultaneously came to a halt. Jenny looked startled and a tiny bit pleased.

And I thought, *She hoped this would happen, and it has. A dance is something she deserves*, and I felt smaller for not having more courage.

She never said yes to Sam, but the look on her face made her answer known.

Sam took her by the arm and guided her into the cultural hall, while Ruth stood in a prominent place at the edge of the dancing area and smiled.

And they danced once, and later that night I danced

with Jenny, and then Bishop Allred danced with her, and not one of us ever had a thought that we had done something that was wrong and required repentance.

I suppose some people talked about Sister Callison and who danced with her. I suppose some of them were bothered by it all, and maybe someone looked up a scripture and another person quoted a General Authority and someone else thought less of Sam, of me, and of our bishop, but it didn't matter. You can find something wrong in almost every picture, and you can find something ugly even in the midst of grace and beauty. It mostly depends on what you set out to look for.

It was the right thing to do that night; it somehow made Jenny Callison feel more complete after her heart had been torn in pieces and the way she looked at herself had been skewed.

Two years later, Jenny Callison met a doctor who was a widower. Together they went to the temple, and to his four children and her two they added two more, and they're still in the area and doing well, and I am sure they will love each other always.

Jenny Callison, mother to eight, and all the promise of her lifetime has bloomed.

Four months ago, when Sam was hospitalized for the first lengthy stay, the doctor who married Jenny came by and visited. He was polite and respectful, and he said, "Thank you for dancing with Jenny first."

Sam and I knew exactly what he meant.

* * *

I huddle in the chair not far from Sam's bed and pull a spare blanket up around my shoulders as a gray chill creeps down my spine. I hear him breathing lightly, slowly. A machine near his bed emits a steady, faint hum. As night grows stronger and the temperature outside swoons, the heater crackles to life and hisses and the blanket drops from my shoulders. In the hallway, I hear hushed voices as a new shift of nurses comes on duty, their shoes squeaking as they begin their first rounds.

And I think how odd it is to be seventy-one and how quickly, how very quickly, all of this happened. No, not just Sam's illness and the doctors' solemn, unwavering diagnoses, but *all of it*. Blink, and I was a boy growing up in a small town in eastern Oregon, fishing with my father high in the Eagle Mountains. Blink, and I was a young man, home from a mission to Great Britain. Blink, and I entered the army and served in Korea and saw many things I wished to never see. Blink, and I had met Helen and our plans were launched. Blink, and I was a father, once, twice, and three times. Blink, and I was beginning my practice, a new attorney almost thirty years old. Blink, and I was at high school orientations and football games on Friday nights. Blink, and my hair began to gray and my body ached more when I came in from gardening or a round of golf. Blink, and parts of my body didn't feel or work like they once did. Blink, and my wife had slowed a step and I had fewer springtimes ahead of me than behind me. Blink again, and most of a lifetime had passed by, and little did it matter that I still felt young in my heart and young in my attitude. It went too fast, just as I heard the prior generation say it would, although I did not believe it until I could look back fifty years or so.

Yet there is comfort in all of this. I would have done very little differently, had I the chance to start over again with the knowledge I now have. I would have spent more time on the floor as the bear chasing my excited and laughing little girls and more time near their bedsides in prayer, because that is when I seemed to pray the best and feelings of thanksgiving washed over me with ease.

I know we are taught to pray in many ways and in almost all situations, but that is the way I most prefer, near a little one as the little one sleeps.

All those years, gone. But I have no strong regrets to blacken the pages already turned, and this brings contentment and peace.

I stand and fold the blanket and walk toward the bed to see if anything has changed. Nothing has. My mind spins, stutters, stalls, and I feel tired again. I take my place on the large chair and close my eyes and dream, this time falling into a fast, deep, and furious sleep.

It is our eldest daughter, Kate, of whom I dream. She is seventeen years old again, tall, her hair long and brown.

"Kate," I say to her, "you are old enough to date. You can go out now. It is an okay thing to do, since you likely will be married to a man someday."

Kate wiggles her nose and scrunches up her face. In the dream, she is lying on her bed and the bright light of a spring day flares into her room.

"Oh, Daddy."

"They do exist, these young men, and while I agree most of them are distasteful and none of them is good enough for you, it would bring your parents some relief for you to at least acknowledge their existence, as unrefined and as unappealing as they are. It will give your mother hope of being a grandmother someday."

"I'm just not that interested." And she slips her hands behind her ears and gracefully pulls her hair back, then straightens her bangs.

"You are a pretty girl. I know some of the boys in the ward would like to go out with you. I have heard talk in the hallways. Priests are not subtle creatures."

"I know, Daddy. They do drop hints, but I'm not

interested in them. Right now they are, you know, boys. Later, maybe I'll change."

"You are so pretty."

She sits up on her bed and looks at me. Kate, in some ways, is the son I never had. She fishes as well as I do, and she is the one who insisted we attach a basketball hoop to the garage. We have spent many afternoons together in the mountains, carefully picking our way up a rocky slope, hiking a trail that will take us to the top of a ridge, where we can look down at a shimmering mountain lake and up at snow-clad peaks and share some water and eat our trail mix and bite into our peanut butter and jam sandwiches. When we sat on those ridges and the wind died and the water didn't shimmer and the whole world, at least the part of it we could see, seemed like a beautiful painting, it was the closest to slowing time I've ever witnessed, though Dr. Einstein would say we needed more speed and gravity to really make it so.

Kate looks away from me and says, "I know I'm pretty." To her, it is a statement of fact, not of arrogance, because Kate is probably the person least disposed toward arrogance of anyone I've ever known. Were she not pretty, she would just as easily say, "I know I am homely," and it would be no different from saying she is pretty. That is the way Kate is. She sees things simply and clearly and deals with situations just as they are.

"How about Kirk Price? He seems like a nice young man."

"Kirk? No, I don't think so. Not for me."

"Chris Ballinger?"

"Too smooth. Too stuck on himself. When I go on a date, I don't want to spend the night listening to someone talk about himself all the time."

"Phillip Anderson?"

"No. Not my kind. Really, Daddy, you are it. You are the only one for me."

While this is the kind of message every father wants to hear and the one that I coached all of my daughters to recite over a period of many years, I know that it someday will become worn and frayed, and some young man will leave my daughter's words in a trash heap on the floor, and then I will be renting tuxedos and planning a trip to the temple and worrying about wedding bells and wedding bills.

It is all part of being a Latter-day Saint and being a father and watching time slip away.

I try once more. "Rob Nicholson?"

Rob is a young man without guile, sweet and honest, and when you look into his eyes you see only good things and warmth, and I don't think he has ever done anything wrong in his life, except at Scout camps, but whatever is done wrong there is quickly forgiven because the Lord knows and understands Boy Scouts. Yet even with his sterling characteristics, I think the girls size up Rob as something of a clod.

"Rob?" Kate stands up. "Rob?" She leaves the room, turning at the door. "Rob?" and she tosses back her hair and giggles at some huge, private joke. Her laughter rings down the hallway.

Helen walks in, having heard the last part of our conversation.

"You can't push Kate," she says.

"I wasn't pushing; I was only suggesting. Fathers can suggest all they want to. It has to do with being a patriarch and can be verified in the discourses of Brigham Young."

"You and Brigham Young. She's not eighteen yet. Kate will be fine."

"I know she will. In the meantime, she is going to cut

the hearts out of some good young men. Cut them out and not even know or maybe not even care."

"Yes, I think she will. You trained her too well as a child that no man is good enough for her."

"Except for her father."

"Yes, except for her father." And we both smile.

That is the way the dream ends, only it wasn't really a dream because a conversation among Kate and Helen and me happened once just like that.

The door opens slowly, and the nurse who will be on duty for the next eight hours comes in. "Hello, Marcus," she greets me.

"Good evening to you, Meredith."

Meredith is in her late forties, quiet and competent. She is a stout woman with large, strong hands. I am glad she is working tonight, because if Sam takes a turn for the worse it is comforting to know that Meredith and her powerful hands are nearby and that she would know exactly the right things to do.

"Any change?"

"None that I can see. He has slept the whole time. I hope that he will wake up for a little while and that I might speak to him. Do you think that is possible?"

Meredith mulls the question. "Yes, it is possible. But I can't say what the chances are or, even if he does wake up, whether he will recognize you."

She peers at Sam, then she looks at me. "You want to say good-bye to your friend, don't you, Marcus? You want to say good-bye to him once more."

"Yes, I want to say good-bye to him. We store up too many good-byes and I love yous and don't say them until it is too late." I look at Sam and realize again how much it means to me that he wakes up, if only for a few seconds, so that I can say good-bye once more. "That is part of the reason I came tonight, for the chance to say good-bye."

"Then we will assume you get your chance. Be ready when it happens, Marcus."

"I will, Meredith. I will know what I should say, if it is only a few words."

She leaves, and I am again alone with my friend and thoughts. Outside, drops of rain tap against the window, and I wonder if there will be snow on the ground in the morning.

CHAPTER SIX

The airplane glides downward. Below me, I see neat farms, green, symmetric, lush, with dozens of lakes scattered across the landscape, their beds scooped out by great, icy hands thousands of years ago. Their waters shine in the early-summer sun, and the whole earth looks green and blue and pleasant. Helen grips my hand as the landing gear rumbles beneath us and the pilot gives last instructions before our final descent.

"So this is Minnesota," I say, because it is the only thing I can think of, although I know it sounds trite.

"Minnesota. Our new home. Maybe," Helen says, her death grip on my left hand now loosened, because our plane has touched down and is coasting to a stop.

We arrived in Minnesota this way: a firm in St. Paul needed an attorney to do some local work where I was then living, and a former classmate of mine gave the attorneys my name. I did the work, and I did it well, and I got along with all of the Minnesota lawyers over the phone and in the conference we held in St. Paul. I thought my end of the business done until I received a phone call inviting Helen and me back to Minnesota to talk about a job.

I didn't know what to say, so all I could say was yes, and besides, Helen and I had never been to Minnesota together, and I thought it might be fun. So Helen's mother came for a visit to watch the girls, and we boarded the plane and flew to the Midwest, where I met with the senior attorneys in the firm and ate dinner with them in nice restaurants, and one attorney's wife took Helen around town shopping and looking at real estate, and we even went to a Minnesota Twins baseball game, and I saw Harmon Killebrew hit a home run.

All in all, we had a glorious time, and the spectacle of a home that sat on the edge of a lake appealed to us. Oh yes, I would earn almost twice as much money too, were I to take the job.

I told them that I needed to go home and talk it over with my family and added that we thought Minnesota was indeed a lovely place and we felt it could become our home.

Then Helen and I flew home, and the real work began.

"It is a nice place, and I had a good time, and I think we could get through the winters okay. They're probably not much more severe than here," Helen said.

"It is a beautiful place," I said.

"Yes, it was nice. We need to talk it over with the girls."

So we did what Mormon families have done from at least the time when parents gathered around a stone fireplace, and the father cleared his throat and said, "We are thinking of a move. It will mean that we must sell our home here and most of our belongings, board a ship, cross the ocean, and then walk another 2,000 miles or so to a place in the desert that probably can't grow crops, and the biggest lake around is so salty that you can't sink in it. Are you with me on this?"

Come to think of it, Father Lehi probably gave almost the same speech as he packed up the family tent, and even Adam had a transfer forced upon him after he partook of a certain apple.

For a group of people who place so much value on family, place, home, and roots, we are very adept at pulling up stakes and moving quickly and often.

So we gathered the girls around, and we took the low road with them, talked about a home on a lake, a boat, fishing and waterskiing, and the better shopping. We told them there weren't all that many LDS people in Minnesota; they'd be badly outnumbered by the Lutherans and Catholics, but that was okay because they were good people and it would give us the chance to be missionaries. "It will be our family adventure. We will be a little bit like the pioneers of old, coming to a new place and unsure of what awaits us there, other than the shopping is good," I said, and while I would not put myself in the category of Lehi, I think I did a pretty fair job of pitching Minnesota to our daughters.

Elizabeth, who was five at the time, liked the idea best of all, especially the part about owning a boat and having a lake in her backyard. She also wanted to make sure her swing set would be coming along.

Debra was more hesitant, but shopping was her soft spot, and the promise that she could come back every summer and maybe over Christmas too turned her our way.

Kate was the most reluctant, because this had been her home for the longest time among our children, but she said, "I will be at college next year, and it doesn't matter where I come home to, as long as my family is there. And I think there is some great canoe country in northern Minnesota, so Dad and I would have a place to go." Then she used that great Mormon throwaway line, tossed at us with what I would term insouciance and maybe a little bit of guile: "Do what you think is right."

Everything had gone just about as well as we could have hoped for, because Helen and I had already pictured ourselves on that boat in the middle of the lake, our three-level home hugging the shoreline, until Kate said that last thing about doing what is right. Trying to figure out what is right almost always complicates things, and Latter-day Saints for the most part don't like to deal with complicated situations; we'd much rather just instantly know what is right and do it, especially if it fit with something we'd heard in the last general conference or in Sunday School the week before.

We spend a lot of effort and energy figuring out what is right, which I suppose isn't a bad use of our time. But sometimes I suspect the Lord would like to tell us, *Either way is right. Just make a choice, and I'll support you, and I'll find good things for you to do, plus a few challenges, no matter what you decide.*

We always want to feel good about things, and I guess that is proper too, although through the years I have had many people look at me from across a desk and tell me with a straight face that they "feel good about it" when they are on the verge of doing something very foolish, such as quitting their job, selling their home, letting a fourteen-year-old go on a date, or leaving their spouse.

We found ourselves in a dilemma about Minnesota, thanks to our eldest child's counsel to do what is right. We thought we wanted to move to Minnesota, all in the name of a great opportunity, but one look at Helen and I knew she was having as many second thoughts as I was, and neither one of us was feeling good about much at all.

So I took my dilemma to Sam.

"What do you think?" I asked him as he teed up the ball on the seventh hole at the public golf course. "Do we become Minnesotans?" From Sam, the wisest man in my circle of acquaintances, I hoped for a quick and clear answer. He'd been listening to my tale of woe for the first six holes, not doing more than nodding and asking an occasional polite question, which I suspected was to prove that he was at least paying a little attention to my problem. Now it was time to put the question to him directly and get his opinion. Do we not receive answers to questions and prayers through messengers? Sam, I hoped, was my messenger.

He looked at me and cleared his throat, and I thought, *What he says next is coming from the Lord because Sam is indeed serving as a messenger.*

And with that buildup, expecting, as it were, manna from heaven, I looked at Sam, and he said, "Beats me, Marcus. It's your call." Then he took his compact and textbook-perfect swing, and the ball bounded down the middle of the fairway. "You're up, partner."

It was two holes later before I finally let him know that I had hoped for more direction. He was just about ready to putt when I expressed my mild disappointment in his answer, and he looked up at me and said, "Marcus, are you trying to freeze me before I putt?"

"No. I have done many things that could be viewed as wrong and sinful, but I would not try to freeze my partner before he putts. I have my standards. I really just wanted to know what you think about our prospective move to Minnesota. I have to let the firm know by the end of the week."

And Sam then proved that he understood me perhaps better than any other human being on the face of the earth, and that includes Helen. He looked at me and said, "All right, Marcus. Why do you want to move to Minnesota? Is it mostly for things?"

I did not like his question, but I had asked for it, and now I had to face the truth. In the next few seconds, I looked long and deep into my heart and found an answer, the answer that had been there all along but that I had ignored. "Yes, if we move to Minnesota, it will be mostly for things, and I know that things cannot bring happiness, and I think too many people in the Church think that things will, even though they would never say it aloud."

Sam putted his golf ball, and it went at least a foot to the right. "Nuts," he said. Then he looked back at me. "Could you leave your mountains?"

I said, "No. I hear there are mountains in northern Minnesota, but I don't think they are real mountains. Montana is the nearest place with real mountains, and it is too far to go to see them. I want my mountains close by."

"Then do you have an answer?"

"I think so. I feel good about my answer."

"Good. I'd hate to break in a new golf partner. Quality partners are hard to find."

I wondered how the women in my life would take my decision, but they didn't break stride when I announced it. Helen extracted a promise to consider a new house in town somewhere, and I believe the girls were all relieved, although the thoughts of glorious and lavish going-away parties and tearful farewells with friends were tucked away deep in a back drawer somewhere.

So we stayed put, and I have never regretted our decision. I am glad that I stayed a small-town lawyer, and I am happy that my roots grow deep in fertile soil.

Because Mormons are generally good people and because we have been taught that blessings follow goodness as the night follows the day, we sometimes think that we should be blessed with things and stuff, big homes, nice cars and good jobs, fancy clothing, and investments that return interest in double or triple digits. When we think that way, we do not see the Lord at work, I believe. He blesses us in ways that are far more subtle and far more profound than we could probably ever imagine on our own, and He does it on His timetable, not ours. Getting ahead has an earthly meaning, and getting ahead can have an eternal meaning, which I think we call progress. And I'd rather progress than get ahead, and I am glad the Lord is sublime because it gives me much to ponder. When I can't fall asleep at night, I think of the sublime blessings in my life and I always feel better, and when it comes my sleep is sweeter.

Minnesota is a wonderful place, I'm sure. But it was not the place for the Hathaway family.

Had we moved, I also would have had to find a new golfing partner, and, as Sam implied, it is a formidable challenge, and I'm not sure I was up to it.

* * *

I push a button on my watch, and the face lights up, and I see that it is now well after midnight. Sleep visited briefly, but now my eyes are open and my mind is running again, and I could no more stop it or slow it down than I could stand at the frothing, white ocean and turn the tide with the vigor of my thought.

After I turned down the job in Minnesota, we built the house that Helen and I had talked about. We had outgrown our home, so a few years later we undertook the greatest challenge a married couple can face. We bought a lot and hired a contractor and began building the home. Through the choosing of paint, tile, trim, window coverings, appliances, and right down to the shower door and the kind of grass we planted, Helen and I talked, argued, discussed, prayed, compromised, and finally just wore ourselves out and reached the point of simply wanting everything done. Through it all, our contractors, Mr. Shields and Mr. Gambaro, were patient and understanding and kept their mumbling to an admirable minimum. Of course, we paid the princely sum of $31,000 for the house, so we figured that they had to put up with our quirks.

Our daughters finally got their going-away party, and it was a wonderful event for them. Tears were shed, and solemn pledges of fidelity were made, and they were only mildly disappointed when their friends hardly ever called them or visited them even though we were fewer than five miles away from our old neighborhood.

The move took us to a new ward, and we started over again in many ways. We promised the Nicholsons that we wouldn't let five miles stand in our way, that we would stay in touch, that we would still visit each other's homes, occasionally go out to dinner, keep up on family birthdays, and in general just continue the way we had for more than a decade.

Of course we were honest and sincere about continuing the same sociality that had existed among the Nicholsons and Hathaways, but when our lives settled into a routine again, the only consistent link between the two families was my weekly golf game with Sam. We still loved the Nicholson family, but for some reason five miles and a ward boundary are about the same as moving to another continent when you are LDS.

Golf, however, endures. This, I think, is proof that golf is eternal and will be played in the next life, although I imagine the language on the course will need to be toned down a bit in the next estate. Although I have no proof that golf is eternal, I believe that if Brigham Young were still around he would be a golfer, if for no other reason than he would need to get away from the house and all those women for awhile. Joseph Smith was tall and athletic by all accounts, and my guess is that he could hammer a golf ball straight and long. I do, though, continue my search for statements in the writings of General Authorities to verify that golf exists in the afterlife. I also believe that there will be no such thing as a triple bogey and that golf balls will skim across water hazards. Perhaps Sam will let me know in a fine and subtle way when he arrives on the other side and has time to scout out a few courses.

"There is only one lot left on our block, and you and Ruth should buy it. We have a nice neighborhood and a wonderful ward, and the sidewalks are curved, and there are nice, little berms in front of many homes," I told Sam as he and I drove to the course for a quick nine holes one evening. "The houses have skylights, and there is a community swimming pool."

Sam had become a principal at one of the junior high schools, and his summer employment, painting homes, kept him more busy than he really wanted. The Nicholsons seemed to be prospering, and I thought they could afford a home in our area.

"I don't think so," he said glumly. "Teacher's salary."

Sam and Ruth were the parents of five children, and maybe curved sidewalks and skylights were out of their range. Something felt a little droopy inside of me because I knew that Sam and Ruth were the best of our friends and I did not like our relationship skinnied down to Christmas cards and swatting golf balls. But I thought it might be uncomfortable to talk about it with him anymore if money were the problem. So I let go of it, except for one last time.

"Only one lot left on our street. Last chance to be neighbors with the Hathaways," I said to Sam one blistering summer afternoon, when I had left the office a little early and sought refuge on the golf course. "Three down from our house. Maybe that is too close for you, although it would make our driving to the golf course much more convenient."

Sam still had flecks of paint in his hair, and he was tired, and it was so hot that you could see the smaller trees sagging and the long blades of grass turning a sickly shade of blue, and in the distance the mountains floated and danced in the heat waves. "I can't even think about it now, Marcus. Like you, we have outgrown our house, but I can't even think about it. I hope to have the strength to finish this round of golf and break 50 doing so."

Three days later the sold sign appeared on the last vacant lot, and again I felt empty and had to tell myself, *It would have been nice, but life is usually not like that, and friends are too often separated, so stop worrying, and try to make some new friends.*

I called Sam, and he was not home. He was still out painting as the evening faded to twilight. Ruth answered.

"I'm very sorry," she said after I told her the news about the last lot. "We would have loved to have been your neighbors. Let us know if a home ever comes up for sale on your street. Maybe it will happen sometime."

I gave her my solemn pledge that I would do so.

A week went by, and I saw one of our builders, Mr. Shields, drive up to the last vacant lot. I said to him, "Good morning. Do you have another building job here?" And he said yes, he did, and he expected the couple to come along in a few minutes. He asked us how we liked our house, and I said we liked it fine, although one of the electrical outlets didn't seem to be working. Mr. Shields said he would send out the electrician to fix it. I was turning away when he said, "Here come your new neighbors now, Mr. Hathaway. Would you like me to introduce them to you?"

I turned to say yes, and then, after seeing the car and its occupants, decided it would not be necessary.

Sam and Ruth drove up, big smiles on their faces, giggling about what they had put over on Helen and me.

And they went through the same thing we did, the arguments, the indecision, the second-guessing, the doubts, the remorse, the counting of each dollar, the nagging, and the feeling that, despite the odds, the home and marriage might just work out after all.

The Nicholsons moved into the home twenty-two years ago, and they have been our neighbors ever since, although all of our other original neighbors have moved on, and some of the houses have gone through three or four owners since then.

It's funny. Back then, we were all young and strong, and Sam and I were nearing the peaks of our careers. And yet we built homes that we would call our last.

Sam's home is mostly built of bricks. It is strong and solid and has held together remarkably well. He painted the trim on it himself only two summers ago. The trees, small and slender two decades ago, are now full and large, and they need to be pruned.

And tonight, I hope that Ruth is resting at least a little in that sturdy, happy house of brick. Sam would like to be there, lying at her side and holding her hand when the sun burst over the eastern hills, if only he could.

Later in the spring, I will prune the trees for Ruth.

CHAPTER SEVEN

Right after we moved into the house, Kate left. She went to college at BYU.

I have now seen my three daughters leave home, and I am not used to it. I still don't like it. Yes, we are on the earth to collect experiences and learn from them, but seeing your children move away is one experience that I wish we could avoid. Families may be forever, but as soon as children are eighteen or so, you begin to wonder just what is meant by that expression.

They come to you sweet and pure and innocent, and when you first see them you learn more about life at that instant than at any other time. You think you are on a long road and that it will never end and that they will always be with you. You think that it is all so wonderful and that you could never know greater joy and that you never want to be called anything other than Dad or Mom. You just begin to think they really are all your own, and then they grow up and they must move on too, and you have to say good-bye, and nothing is ever quite the same, and you ache for the sweetness of days gone by.

You find the road does have an end. You come to a canyon, and you must stop and let out one of your family members, and then you drive ahead, and never again does the road seem so straight and long, and you worry always about when the next canyon appears.

And it breaks your heart.

This is how I feel about watching my children leave home.

It is the night before we take Kate to school. She is quiet as she gathers the last of her essential belongings. For the last two weeks, she has selected what she will need at school and carefully packed it in boxes. At first the pile of boxes was small at the top of the stairway that led from our basement. It grew each day, I noticed as I returned home from work. The larger the pile, the closer our good-bye, and I came to resent the pile of boxes and tried not to look at it because it reminded me that something was changing, and I really didn't like this part of my journey very much.

Then comes the time when I must pack the boxes in our station wagon, and I do okay until I see the box with her pots and pans and old silverware, and I think, *It wasn't so long ago that she was playing house with her little, plastic pots and pans and silverware,* and I lose it, big tears plunge down my face, and I start sobbing right there in the garage while Kate is upstairs straightening her room and Helen is at the store buying a few last-minute items for our daughter who is leaving.

It is the second time I have cried since becoming an adult, the first being at John Parsons's funeral. And I feel so very much alone.

Kate comes to the garage with her suitcase, and if this were the movies or I were the kind of father who is always wise, I would say something to her that she would always remember, that would make her load light because it is a moment primed for teaching.

I try to distill all that I know and all that she should know into a few memorable sentences, but I cannot think of anything because life is too complicated to pare to a few lean statements; I feel like I have just taken a called third strike with the bases loaded in a World Series game. All I can manage to say is, "Do you have everything that you will need?"

And Kate looks at me and says, "Yes, I have everything I need. You and Mother have prepared me well."

Then I feel better because I understand that there is more than one level to my question, and Kate assumes I have spoken allegorically.

"Good," I say. "I also think you have all that you need. We have trained you to the best of our ability. Now it is time to try out the things that you know and believe and see how they square with the real world. Sometimes you will hurt, and sometimes you will be discouraged, and sometimes you will long for things that are more simple, but this is all part of why we came here. You will also find joy along the way, and that's what you should remember, especially when you fall down and your knees get bloody. I will miss you, Kate, and I will always love you, and I would do anything for you if I thought it was right for you."

Kate pushes her suitcase to me. "I know, Daddy."

And I feel the part of a wise father after all, although I recognize that I stumbled into the role, which is often the case when we feel wise. I am no Ward Cleaver, that is for sure.

We leave the next morning, early, an hour before the sun rises. Debra and Elizabeth are in the back of the station wagon asleep, with Kate, wide-eyed, looking at everything for the last time in a long while, even our garage, and every home on our street. Helen sits by me, and she is quiet, and soon her eyes are closed, though I do not think she sleeps.

So our journey begins, and every mile seems to say to me, *This is a trip of sadness, and you will be with one less*

*member of your family when you return. Roads lead home, and
they also lead away, but you are taking part of you away. There
will be times when you lead your loved ones home, and you should
remember that too.*

We push into the first dewy light of morning, the
mountains to my right and left looking worried and concerned. In some of the narrow-cut canyons, I see that the
aspens are splashy with gold, yellow, and red, and it seems
that autumn is the only fitting time to take away your
daughter and leave her at school, because autumn is a time
when we say good-bye to so much and slowly watch the
world about us fade from jade to gold to brown to gray.

I drive relentlessly, as most fathers do, in an effort to
make good time, as if any of us can make time at all, much
less good time or bad time. It is early afternoon, and our
trip is more than half over, and I feel pleased until the purpose of our travels comes to mind and sinks into my soul.
We need to get Kate to school in time for a dormitory orientation tonight and then a freshman orientation in the
morning, and sometime in the mix of the day we need to
buy her books and go shopping with her for a few of life's
necessities, such as toothpaste and soap and potato chips.
In a place where the mountains recede far from the road
and there is a long, wide plain sweeping away as far as we
can see, our car shivers, sputters, gasps, and dies.

"What's wrong?" Helen asks, and the girls in the backseat are now wide awake, and questions are in their eyes
too.

"Something is wrong with the engine," I say matter-
of-factly.

I am not much of a mechanic. Engines are a world
unknown. I know that somehow, when I turn the key and
I have oil and gas in my car, the up-and-down motion of
the pistons is transferred to the wheels of the car, and it

moves ahead. What the problem is with my car at this moment, I haven't a clue. When your car stalls and stops, it is a defining moment for any man, especially a Latter-day Saint husband and father who is also a patriarch, a person who should not only lead his family spiritually but should also be able to overhaul his car engine in a couple of hours on a Saturday afternoon.

"I'll check under the hood," I say. "I think it is the electrical system." So I amble to the front of the car, trying to project confidence and hoping I can reach under and find the gizmo that unlatches the hood. Fortunately, I find it and open the hood and stick my head under it, where my face is blocked from the view of my family and I can look as confused and perplexed as I really feel. I see nothing that looks out of place. I hear one of our car doors open and am joined by Kate.

"Do you know what is wrong?"

"No, I don't," I say and mumble a little under my breath, which is something all men do when they look at engines; I think it is something in our genetic code.

At this moment, I think of Sam, who is good with his hands and would know exactly what to do. I envy him. He is a true patriarch.

Kate wanders off. I stare at the engine for at least fifteen minutes, all the while growing more tense because we need to have our daughter to school at a certain time and we don't have much of a margin to work with.

The car windows are rolled down because it is warm, and I hear Helen comforting our two younger daughters, telling them everything will be fine, and making a game out of how many different state license plates they see as cars zoom by us. In my heart, though, I know they are all thinking, *If he were more like Adam or Lehi, he'd know what to do and we'd be out of this pickle in no time. Nephi set up a smelter and forged steel, then built a ship in a barren wilderness, but this fellow is stumped by a silly combustion engine. If Nephi could see this, he would shake his head and think,* "He is a good man, but I'm glad he wasn't on the ship with me. He never would have made it in the New World."

Then I hear footsteps behind me, and they belong to Kate.

"Look at what I found!" she exults. "Wildflowers. Little, purple flowers with white in the center. Wildflowers. They're in that swale over there. Can you believe it? Purple and white, and they're still in bloom, and it's almost fall."

She sighs and looks happy.

And I think, *I am proud to have a daughter who finds flowers near the road when the car is broken down. I am proud that she knows what a swale is.*

I say, "But you may be late. I don't have any idea about what is wrong with the car."

She says, "I know. I don't care. It doesn't matter. Just look at these flowers. I'll show them to Mom, and then she'll know everything will be okay."

I do not understand the connection between wildflowers in bloom and cars that are not running, but I too feel that everything will be all right. In a world where wildflowers bloom in September, a car can be made to run again. Kate exudes confidence, and it wraps itself around me.

"I think we have some water and paper towels, and I'll wrap the flowers so that I can put them in my room tonight."

She walks back to her mother and sisters. Overhead a flock of Canada geese fly, going toward a new home far away, squawking, flapping, following an order of nature as old as the earth itself. I see something in their situation and something in mine about geese and people needing to move on. And ever since that time, now almost twenty-five years later, when I see Canada geese I think of Kate and wildflowers and stopping on the road and seeing beautiful, sweet desert flowers.

I hear the scrunch of tires on the side of the road and look up to see a man and his wife and two sons in the backseat. He smiles and jumps out of his car, and I say to myself, *I do not know this man, but I love him and all he stands for.*

"Car troubles?"

"Yes."

"I'm a pretty good mechanic. Mind if I have a look?"

"Not at all. I'm stumped. But it doesn't take much to stump me."

He pokes his head under the hood. His sons climb out of the car, tall, red-haired, and handsome. They mumble. In less than thirty seconds, he says, "Your fan belt snapped." His sons nod in agreement.

"Can that be fixed here?"

"Maybe."

My testimony that there is a kind and loving Heavenly Father and that he hears our prayers and knows us increases dramatically on the spot.

"Do you have hose in your car?"

"Like a garden hose?"

"No. Like what women wear."

"I have four women in my car. We can find hose."

A quick call for hose yields a pair from Helen, although she is highly skeptical. "And they're called hosiery, and I paid three dollars for them. Are you sure they can be used to fix the car?"

"I am most certain. Trust me. A small and trifling price, this three dollars of yours. This will work," I say, and

I imagine Nephi and Lehi having a change of opinion about me. Then I say aloud, opaquely, "If I needed to, I could build a smelter right here and forge steel."

The man under the hood takes the hose, mumbles a bit more, and says, "This might work. I've done it once before. You wrap the hose tight, and it will buy you twenty, thirty miles. That should get you to Tremonton, and any filling station should be able to help you from that point."

I am soon back in the car. My roadside angel gives me the signal, his two sons grin, I turn the key, and the engine roars.

"I'll follow you to Tremonton," he says. "That way, I'll know you are safe." He looks at Kate and Debra and Elizabeth. "Off to the Y?"

"Yes, we are."

"First time?"

"Yes."

"Not easy. William is our third. We have six more at home. Grandmother Shurtz is watching them."

"Thank you. Thanks so much." Then I clumsily try to shove a twenty-dollar bill his way, but he laughs and pushes away my hand. "We all rely on others sometimes, don't we? If my car is broken down on the way back, stop and help me. Or if you don't see me, stop and help someone else."

And I have tried to do just that many times, in honor of my friend whose name I never learned. He drove an Oldsmobile with Oregon plates, and he is a good man. That is all I know about him.

Now that I am old, I wonder about that man and his family and his son William, who helped us with the car, and I hope they have had a good and healthy life. I think in the next life there will be a directory, and all you will need to do is say, "I'd like to check up on that fellow who helped us when our car conked out when we took Kate to school." And right away I'll know what happened to him, maybe even get the chance to say hello and thank him again.

The rest of our trip was uneventful, although that is not a good choice of words. It was actually filled with events, important family events, things that are pressed into my mind as though they happened last week. I see Kate dragging her trunk into her dorm room. I see her meeting her roommate for the first time and remember the feeling that I had, *Please, Lord, let this work between them.* I see the trip to the grocery store and spending fifty dollars more on food than we had planned because I wanted her never to be hungry. I see the frenzied trip through the canyon of texts in the bookstores. I see the moment when she had to say good-bye because she had to attend the dorm meeting and when I knew that this was the end of one thing and the beginning of another, and I remember how worried I was because I was less a part of what was to come in her life. I see Helen crying and the long, tear-stained faces of our other daughters in the backseat of the station wagon as we made our sad trip home.

I see my hands gripping the steering wheel, the long road home at night, turning into our driveway at three A.M. when the moon was bright and clear and the Milky Way was stunning and the mountains to the north were shadowy, purple, their outlines crisp in the clear night air. I see the girls waking and hear my voice saying, "We're home," and Debra rubbing her eyes and saying, half-asleep, "But Kate isn't here, and it doesn't seem as much like home anymore," and silently seconding her sentiment, and wondering if the dull ache in my heart would ever subside.

And I remember feeling so incomplete, because until I became a father I had not known what it is to be whole.

And I remember looking back one final time as we pulled out of the parking lot at the dormitory and seeing Kate wave to us, her eyes red and brimming with tears and a passel of purple and white wildflowers cradled in her left hand.

And the funny thing is, I want to do it all over again, and sometimes in my prayers I ask for the chance and hope that in God's great plan of limitless creations that once more I will hold in my arms a baby girl I can call my own.

In the hospital hallway, someone pushes a cart, and the wheels squeak and scratch and bring me back to the present. *This is your life, and it has been good and it has been hard too. You never knew how hard it would be, and maybe that is for the best,* I say to myself. It is now almost three in the morning. A maintenance worker walks by, his keys jangling from his belt.

After I returned home from taking Kate to college, I talked with Sam. I told him how I felt the void, the emptiness, the helpless feeling that something sweet had gone by too quickly. He nodded and listened, then put his hand on my left shoulder, then nodded and listened some more.

"I am sorry for you, Marcus. We've been through that too with our oldest daughters, and I know how difficult it is."

We stood in his garage in the soft twilight of that September day. The sun was almost done with its day's work, and it lobbed its lazy rays up Sam's driveway and into his garage door. Specks of dust danced and twirled in the sunlight, and the dry fragrance of dropped leaves and coolness enveloped us. Sam seemed a little tired, and his head drooped like a flower in a heavy rain.

"When you have sons, they go away to college or the military or they take jobs in other places," he said. "And they serve missions too, and you do not see them for two years. I wonder about saying good-byes. I think it is something for us to learn while we are here. To say good-bye with grace, always trusting that they'll come home again."

He was polishing his golf clubs. Sam Nicholson had the best-kept golf clubs I've ever seen. They always looked new and shiny. He put down his driver.

"By the way, did I tell you about Rob? He got his call yesterday. I would have told you sooner, but you got back so late last night, and I thought you were sleeping in this morning. He is going to Argentina on his mission."

* * *

I am a man who does not have sons, so I can only guess what it feels like to ordain a boy an elder, buy two practical suits and seven white shirts, look for sturdy shoes that can last through thousands of miles of walking in bad weather, hug him, kiss him, and then say good-bye to him for two years. I can only guess and I can only imagine, but I am sure of this: It is a difficult thing to do, and it tears your heart into little pieces that are whipped away in a cold north wind.

We send our sons away for two years, and they are almost always sweet and innocent when they leave, and if all works out well they come home still sweet and innocent but with the testimony of a lion and experiences that will help them navigate through the rest of their lives.

I think a mission is where the subtle and beautiful transformation toward becoming a patriarch begins to unfold. They leave as boys, and they come home as men, but it is a good passage, and there is no mourning over lost youth, only joy when they come home whole and clean and happy.

And while two years is a long time, at least we aren't asked to tie our son to an altar or send our son to save a world that is hard and doesn't think it needs to be saved.

Rob's missionary sacrament meeting, what they used to call farewells back then—and I'm not sure we'll ever quite get over calling them that—was what you would expect from the Nicholsons. It was warm and smart, tender, insightful, and no one spoke for very long, which is still the ultimate measure of a good sacrament meeting to most Latter-day Saints. Then Rob was away, and while I knew Sam and Ruth were proud of him, I also know they worried about him every minute he was gone.

"Hear from the elder lately?" I'd ask Sam in his yard or strolling down a fairway.

"Two weeks ago, and he's doing fine. He is teaching a family named Morales, and he's excited. When you baptize a whole family, you get very excited," Sam would say.

Still, you would not need to look very far into his eyes to see the longing and feel the hollowness as he spoke of his son.

It is not easy to watch your children go away, even when the cause is good and just.

Around that time, another change in calling happened in the Nicholson family.

Bishop O'Dell had served for five years by then, and he seemed tired, and there were more lines on his face, and people in the ward who had been around longer than we had said, "He has worked so hard. He has been a good bishop. But it is time for a change, and I hope the stake presidency gets the message soon."

So the rumors flew, and before stake conference and ward conference everyone was sure a change would be made, and attendance was high at both meetings, but Bishop O'Dell was still our bishop at the conclusion of those meetings. I'm certain that over the dinner table and over pillows at night, talk of a new bishop flowed freely, and mental lists were made, and people said things like,

"I'll support whoever is called, but I sure hope it is not Brother So-and-so, because I couldn't tell him my problems if I needed to, and besides Harriet talks too much."

Latter-day Saints can't or at least shouldn't gamble or drink or smoke, and while we're happy to obey these commandments and life is probably much better for them, we can't resist speculation, especially when a new bishop is about to be called. It is one of the few sneaky things we can get away with, although I'm sure it is something we should repent of, but it is not too terribly high on most peoples' list. I do not think that speculating on who will be the new bishop can keep an otherwise righteous person out of the celestial kingdom, although I'm not sure if even Brigham Young had much to say on the subject.

Well, all of this went on for several months, and the tension grew, and I noticed some men wearing nice, pressed, white shirts a little more often than before and answering more than their share of questions in the Gospel Doctrine class, which I suppose is part of human nature. One Sunday, our stake president strolled in just before sacrament meeting started, and I wondered if several of our ward members were going to survive the experience. But he was just there to say hello and not do much else. At the end of the day, Bishop O'Dell was still our bishop.

Then came the announcement at the end of a sacrament meeting that the stake presidency would be visiting next week to conduct some important business. "Conduct important business" can mean only one of two things to Latter-day Saints: either a ward boundary will change or a new bishop will be called, and everyone knew exactly what was coming in this case. Even the little children stopped fidgeting and the babies miraculously ceased their fussing when Bishop O'Dell, who had a funny look on his face, made the announcement. At the end of the day,

Bishop O'Dell was still our bishop, and we loved him for who he was and how hard he worked, but we knew we could not say that he would still be our bishop in another week.

Changing bishops is a traumatic experience. It is part coronation, part celebration, part wake, part relief, and for some part disappointment. We make too much of it and talk about it more than we should, but speculating about leadership changes is part of our culture, and I don't think it will change anytime soon before the Second Coming.

And I do not stand apart as being perfect in this matter. Helen and I talked more than once about who would be the new bishop.

We talked about several men, and we concluded in each case that they would all be fine bishops. My philosophy at that time in my life was, "Anyone would be a fine bishop as long as that anyone isn't me," and it was a very good way of looking at it. Not that I was like Jonah and trying to run away from any duties, but I wanted to put on a few more years and gain more wisdom before I sat on the stand every Sunday and looked solemn and tried to keep a ward of five hundred people all headed in pretty much the right direction.

Helen said, as I was standing at the sink washing dishes while she was drying, "Do you think you could be called to be the bishop?"

I thought about this for a moment and said, "No, I do not think I will be called because I do not have any feelings about becoming a bishop, and I think the Spirit would have been working me over pretty hard by now if my new first name were to become Bishop. And besides, I do not want to be a bishop. It seems like a great deal of work, and while I am sure there are many blessings, I would rather sit by your side during sacrament meeting each Sunday."

Helen smiled at this, and I think she was pleased. For some women, it is important for their husbands to serve in callings of great responsibility, but all things considered Helen wanted me home most of the time, where I could help with the dishes and help rear our daughters and occasionally take her out for an evening without resorting to calling it date night.

No one from the stake president's office called that week, and I slept well and thought only once or twice about what the new bishop must be going through. On Sunday I wore a pale-blue shirt to church and was very relaxed and feeling smug.

There is no other feeling in the Church like sacrament meeting on the day when a new bishop is to be sustained.

Someone probably will do a study someday about how to spot the new bishop by the time the opening hymn is sung, but I already know. First you look at who is wearing a clean, pressed, white shirt, and that is your starting point. Next you find someone who is sitting quietly in the congregation and not up and smiling and shaking everyone's hand. You also look to see if he has a new haircut and if he looks as though he is about to become ill. If members of his extended family are sitting by him, that is almost the sure sign.

Children are also good indicators. If they are young, they will look fresh-scrubbed and dressed to the nines. If they are teenagers, they will look disappointed, because the new bishop is only their dad and they secretly wish that it were someone a little more with it, and they understand that they will be singularly referred to as "the bishop's kid" for the next few years. If they are girls, it means fewer dates because guys don't often want to go out with the bishop's daughter, because he is the man who is going to go into some detail about moral cleanliness during the young man's birthday interview. If the bishop has teenaged sons, it becomes a case of a crimped social life because they don't dare even hold hands on a date without fear of being reminded by the young woman that their behavior is inappropriate for a bishop's son.

But the key, I believe, is to look at the face of the soon-to-be bishop's wife. She will be smiling, but it will be a forced smile, even if she is one of those good sisters who desire that her husband serve as a bishop. The reality of the calling is about to hit her, and that is why she suddenly is having second thoughts about the whole thing, because she is beginning to realize that she will be a woman alone for much of the next three, four, five, or six years, and there is precious little glory ahead of her, and getting the children ready alone for the first block on a Sunday is not much of a spiritual experience.

These and a thousand other thoughts weigh heavily on her mind, because she feels a little bit like a pioneer whose husband just conked out somewhere along the North Platte, and she realizes that she alone will need to pull the handcart the last thousand miles into the valley.

So on that Sunday, with all those thoughts in mind, I looked around, and it very quickly became apparent to me who our next bishop would be:

Samuel Joseph Nicholson.

And so when President Walker stood at the podium and thanked and praised Bishop O'Dell, and we all raised our hands to show our appreciation, it was absolutely no surprise when Sam's name was read and he and Ruth took those fine, slow, measured steps toward the front of the congregation. And it seemed right and good to call him Bishop Nicholson, and I was happy for him and proud to be his friend, and I knew he would be a great bishop.

And over the next five years, he was indeed a great bishop.

I managed to reach him before he was ushered into the high council room to be set apart. I wanted to offer my congratulations. He saw me as he was beginning to shake hands with the stake presidency members, and he immediately broke away from them. He started to say something about why he had called Brother Martin and Brother Jamison as counselors and not me, but I shook my head and smiled and told him that no explanation was due, that I knew he did only as he was directed by inspiration. He looked relieved, and I realized that the thought that I might be hurt had troubled him and that he had planned to pull me aside after he was sustained and talk with me.

The stake president beckoned him into the high council room, and he and Ruth, the Martin and Jamison families, and an assortment of children and other family members shuffled into the room. The door closed, and with me waiting outside Sam was set apart as the president of the Aaronic Priesthood, as the presiding high priest in the ward, and as a bishop. And before all of that, he was ordained a high priest.

"You are not fine and you are not old, but you are a high priest now," I said to him on the following Saturday morning, as we met at our mailboxes. "But I imagine the fine and the old part of the equation will come to you now, probably at an accelerated rate, because you are an ordained Mormon bishop."

We had ourselves a nice laugh over that, standing there on a happy morning of yellow and blue, the grass wet and fragrant, and the sense of new roads opening before him.

My road would also soon take me to new places. Three weeks later, I wore a white shirt into President Walker's office and was asked to serve on the high council. I agreed to do so, and three days later Sam placed his hands upon my head and ordained me a high priest. And when he hugged me after the ordination was over, he whispered, "Now we both have to work on only the fine and old parts. We're still just kids, aren't we, Marcus?"

Six months later, I asked Sam how it was to be a bishop.

He looked at me for a few seconds eye-to-eye and thought over the question. "It is hard. It is much harder than I thought, but I am trying my best and will always do so," he said.

That is the only time we discussed his calling. Almost fourteen years later, when I was well into my calling as a bishop, I knew what he meant about it being difficult and the need to try hard always.

Before our respective callings as bishops were completed, I would lose most of my hair and Sam's bushy, beautiful hair would fade from blonde to copper to silver. We both would add an impressive array of wrinkles and put on a little weight because there was so little time to exercise, and even if there was time we were too tired to hardly move. We held people in our arms and cried with them, soared when a new baby was born in the ward, walked with people into their Gethsemanes, and unwillingly left them when their Gethsemanes were so difficult that they felt they could not emerge. We helped send missionaries to the world, laid our hands upon the heads of the faithful and prayed that our minds and hearts would be filled with the right things to say, spoke at funerals, talked and taught a lot about repentance, and wondered all along if we were doing everything we could and should, and hoped that no one felt unwanted or unloved.

We died a little each time someone made a serious

mistake or got hurt or went through painful experiences. We walked with them as far as we could, then told them gently that some roads they must walk alone. We were surprised at how often we also felt alone, because a bishop must carry so much by himself, except when he prays.

And I think that every bishop is a hero to me.

I don't know. We ask so much of our bishops, and they really are for the most part just plain guys, and most of them didn't really want the calling anyway but happened to be worthy, and the Lord tapped them on the shoulder when they didn't expect it.

I think I was a good bishop, but when I was released a sense of relief and emptiness washed equally over me, and I was happy to see Bishop Robinson sit in the place I previously occupied. And I watched from the congregation as people swarmed toward our new bishop and his counselors, which is how it should be, because every bishop needs to be loved by his congregation. Only one person came directly to me, arms held wide, his thanks pouring forth.

As you would guess, it was Sam.

CHAPTER EIGHT

I am not sure of the time. A thin line of crimson will soon drape itself over the crest of the mountains. I could look at my watch but choose not to. In the residential area to the south of the hospital, a few lights flicker on. For some, the day shift is beginning.

Meredith walks in and stands in the corner, and I welcome her company as the night grows restless and begins to move away.

"Anything different with our patient?"

"No. Quiet since you were last here. I may have dozed a little, but I would have awakened if he so much as turned."

"For the kind of duty you're pulling, Marcus, dozing is allowed."

"Can he hear us, and if he can hear us, can he understand what we are saying?"

"I don't know, and I don't know. How is that for a sound medical answer? My guess is that he is more aware of his surroundings than we think," she said. Then she sat down in the less-comfortable of the two chairs in the room. "Still hoping to talk with him, aren't you?"

"Yes."

"You'll talk with him whether he is awake or not. I believe he will hear you. Some things I know, even though science doesn't explain them very well. Think up a good speech, Marcus, and then deliver it."

"I will. I was a lawyer for forty years, and I grew to like words. I have given many speeches, but maybe none as important as this. When you say good-bye, it must be just right."

"I guess so. Can't say that I've ever become fond of saying good-bye."

She pulled a blue sweater closer around her. "He had a call an hour ago. A fellow named Wayne just wanted to know how Sam was doing. I said he was resting comfortably but just holding his own, and I know that I broke the rules, but this fellow calls every day, and I feel like he is family if he shows that much concern. He thanked me, and that was that. The call came a little past four. He said he always got up that early."

"Wayne Naught does get up early all the time. He is an old friend, and you're right, he is pretty much family. He calls getting up at six sleeping in," I said.

"Got to get back to work now. I'll check in once more. You know what to do if he gets ornery and changes in some way."

"I do know what to do. I run down the hallway shouting your name."

Meredith smiled briefly and gave me a wink. "That should get things started." She stood, then walked quietly from the room, her white walking shoes squeaking on the floor.

I walked over to Sam. "If you can hear me, Sam, I want you to know that Wayne Naught called again. I don't think he's missed a day yet. He calls me at home some evenings too. You can count on only a few things in life, but one of them is Wayne Naught. He is also your friend, Sam. Wayne Naught would do anything for you."

Wayne Naught. There is only one Wayne Naught.

* * *

Sam and I are walking toward the Naught home. One of Sam's counselors is out of town, and the other is at home coughing, wheezing, and generally getting licked by the flu, and Sam says he just had a revelation and needs my help.

"What kind of a revelation, bishop?" I ask over the phone.

"Just an ordinary one. Kind of a run-of-the-mill revelation," Sam says.

"Can you share the revelation with me?"

"I can and I will, when I pick you up. I'll back the car out in ten minutes, and you be there. Please put on a tie too."

We drive to the Naught home, and all Sam will tell me is that he needs to extend a calling and that he is sure it is the right calling and that it needs to be done, although it has taken the whole month for the Spirit to convince him of it.

"Does this calling concern Nina?" I ask. Nina is Wayne's wife, and she is a jewel, sweet, humble, hard-working, and just plain nice. Wayne is none of these things, except for the hard-working part.

Wayne is a big man with a large head and a huge forehead that turns red when he is angry, which is most of the time. You can see the blood veins on his forehead, squiggly, blue lines like rivers on a map. His hands are wide and meaty and look like they could wrap themselves around a tree with fingertips to spare.

He is a master of scowling, of acting disinterested, and he can cut you off at the knees with one piercing look. He has run off more than his share of home teachers, bishops, and other assorted fools who had dared to tread on his property, much less tried to enter the circle of his life. The records show he is a member, but it is the only evidence we have, either by action or word-of-mouth, that he was ever really immersed by one who held the priesthood. Baptism is probably the only time in Wayne Naught's life that anyone ever had him at a physical disadvantage, and his confirmation was surely a unique experience when others placed their hands upon his head and he did not break arms or jaws in retaliation.

In short, Wayne Naught is an imposing and intimidating man, not given to things of the Spirit. He owns a small trucking company. I wonder if Sam wanted me along in case legal questions should arise regarding assault and battery.

We knock at the door. It is a Tuesday night, and Nina Naught answers. For all of Wayne's roughness, Sister Naught is a perfect counterbalance. She is small, bright-eyed, dressed nicely but not too nicely, quiet, and faithful. She sits in the same pew every week for sacrament meeting with her children, Petey, Marilyn, and Candace.

"Oh! It's you, Bishop and Brother Hathaway. Are you here to see me?"

"Good evening, Sister Naught. No, we are here to see your husband."

She looks very anxious and in her sweet manner seems to be asking, *Are you out of your minds?* Instead, she lowers her voice and says, "You mean Wayne?"

"Yes. Wayne. Your husband," Sam answers confidently.

Now, if Sister Naught had been asked to sell her possessions and begin the trek eastward to Missouri, she would not have blinked an eye but would have immediately gone to work on a huge yard sale. But two priesthood holders visiting her husband unannounced was a test of her faith.

"He's watching The Red Skelton Hour. We never interrupt him when he does that. It's best not to. It's his favorite show."

That sounds like reason enough for me: a large man known for his quick temper is watching his favorite TV show in the sanctity of his own home, and we are there I suspect to call him to repentance. I take a half-step back, but Sam is on a mission.

"We would still like to visit him," he says.

"Okay," she relents, but she looks more nervous now than before.

We walk into the living room, where Red Skelton flickers on a screen before us. He is acting like a seagull, and the audience is roaring, and I think, *If I can just sit down and say nothing and enjoy Red Skelton with Wayne, I may survive this.*

Wayne looks at us, glares, and then grunts. Nina sits uncomfortably on a couch in the corner, across the room from where her husband sprawls in a large chair.

Sam takes a breath, and I realize he also is nervous.

"Hello, Wayne. I am Sam Nicholson, your bishop."

Wayne says nothing. He gazes straight ahead.

Nina looks very worried. An awkward ten seconds or so passes, then Sam begins again. And when he speaks, I am amazed at what he says, and I wonder if my friend is insane or simply a man of God who has an errand to perform.

"Wayne, it is time for you to turn off the television set and listen to us. You are a man who appreciates straight talk, and I am here to give you a dose."

Now Sam has Wayne's attention. Wayne turns his big head toward us, and I feel like prey on the African savanna. He rumbles around in his chair, stands up, and scowls a scowl that would reduce most men to mush. Sam doesn't flinch. Wayne doesn't touch the TV set. Red Skelton is unaware of what is taking place, and I wish I were in the audience laughing at him.

Wayne blinks, and I have never before been happy to see someone blink, but I am now.

"Then talk!" he barks at Sam.

"Wayne, this is what I have to say to you, even though you may not like it. You need to come to church. You need to sit with your wife there and hold her hand, and you need to put your arms around your children and tell them you love them. You need to give up your bad habits and start paying your tithing. You need to be nicer, because you will not be allowed in the celestial kingdom unless you are nice, and I know this supposes that you know what the celestial kingdom is and that you want to take up residence there someday. You need to be ordained an elder and go to the temple, because right now your wife is ready and you are not. You need to be sealed in the temple. You need to become a leader in the Church and put your power to good works instead of using it to frighten people. And you also need to read your scriptures and have family prayer. There are other things, but I will save them for a later conversation. And I say all these things because I am supposed to and because I am your friend."

And I think, *What other things? What more can Sam say? We are dead men.*

Wayne leans forward in his chair, and his large, thick eyebrows are knit together. The blue creeks and streams on his forehead are now rushing, raging rivers. He flexes his fists, and darkness washes over his features.

I experience a feeling that life as I know it is about to end. Wayne tries to talk but can't, and it is probably a good thing because the language would have been the kind usually reserved only for construction sites, military operations, and golf courses. His face turns from pink to red to a deep, rich crimson.

"And there is one more thing," Sam speaks again,

placidly now, and I am ready to side with Nina in her likely opinion about the relative mental stability of our bishop.

"What?" sputters Wayne, the first intelligible word he has spoken in the last few minutes.

"I also extend to you a calling to be the Scoutmaster, because you would be a good one, and Petey is twelve, and I think you are the right kind of man to work with boys."

Now, being a Scoutmaster is a true test of your gospel beliefs. It is not a place for the faint of heart or poor of spirit to serve. I have known good men, well-grounded in the gospel, who were brought to tears and left scarred by the calling of Scoutmaster. I believe that, other than General Authorities, early-morning seminary teachers, and perhaps homemaking leaders, there will be a higher percentage of people who are exalted in the celestial kingdom who were Scoutmasters than just about any other calling. Had Scouts been part of the Church 150 years ago, I believe that Brigham Young would have agreed with me on this point of doctrine.

But at this moment, Wayne is not ready for exaltation and, for that matter, probably not any part of the celestial kingdom. Were I the judge, I would peg him somewhere in the lower third of the terrestrial kingdom and sinking fast as he turns an ever darker shade of red, his wife turns even paler, and strange and corrosive words pour from his mouth.

I think, *The earth is going to split open and yawn, and we are going to be swallowed up in it, and then it will close and there never will be a record of how we all went, other than it had something to do with a visit to the Naught home and interfering with him watching The Red Skelton Hour. There will be a long investigation that will conclude that we all died from natural causes, and no one will ever suspect that the jaws of hell are agape and that we perished when Wayne Naught clamped them shut.*

"Well, Brother Naught, what do you say?" Sam asks politely, as though he were questioning a neighbor about whether he thought it would rain or not.

Wayne stands up and stomps to the front window and stares. His back is turned from us. He says nothing.

Sam clears his throat and calmly asks, "You love your son, don't you?"

Wayne remains with his back toward us, and he doesn't break his gaze for another full minute. Then he turns around, and what I see is one of the greatest surprises of my life.

Wayne Naught, a bear of a man with beetle brows, a barrel chest, the disposition of dynamite, and a hair-trigger temper, a man in command of every situation, who fears nothing except the word *love*, as it turns out, looks at us, and he is crying.

And in a becoming and gentle voice, he says, "Oh, bishop. That's not fair. You know I do."

And in that moment a life is changed. A man who was wayward and hard and harsh becomes a spiritual man because his bishop asks him if he loves his boy.

Nina is still, but tears lace her face too. I can tell her thoughts, and they are very close to these: *I cannot believe this is happening. I have prayed and wondered all these years, and now the sorrow of my heart is lifting because someone else loves Wayne, too.*

Wayne Naught accepted the calling to be our Scoutmaster, and there was no better man for the job. Long after Petey left on a mission, Wayne still led boys to the mountains and returned home with young men. He was a Scoutmaster for eleven years, and boys and young men and young fathers still bless and glorify his name. He reared a generation of good Scouters and more. As a Scoutmaster, he was in the class of Sam Nicholson, and that says a lot.

"Were you nervous in there?" I asked Sam as we drove away from the Naught home that night.

"Yes, but only for a little while. Then it was all calm and all good."

In the hospital room, I look toward the east, where the stars are beginning to dim and the barebacked outline of the mountains is now discernible. In less than an hour, the sun will peek over their highest reaches and a new day will fly to the west.

"Wayne Naught called you, bishop. Your lives honor one another."

I hope Sam heard my message.

* * *

My watch shows it is almost six, and outside the room I hear a cart filled with medicines being pushed down the hallway.

The ring of the phone jars me fully awake. I expect it to be Ruth, up after a restless night of trying to sleep and inquiring about how Sam is doing, with a promise to be at the hospital before much longer. Instead, the voice on the other end of the phone belongs to Helen.

"Made it through the night, the both of you?" she asks.

"Yes, both still accounted for, although I am sleepy. When I get home, I would like to rest, if I can. My mind has been running tonight, and I have been thinking of stories."

She has slept with me for more than forty years, and she knows that when I say my mind is running and I am thinking of stories, I cannot sleep.

"You and those stories. You see much of life as stories. Just for a while stop seeing those stories and get some rest. The kids are coming today. I'll pick them up at the airport just before noon, so it will be quiet and you should be able to get some sleep before they arrive. No change in Sam?"

"No change. He has barely stirred. I hope that he will awaken, and one of the nurses said it is still possible, in her opinion. I worked on a speech off and on last night, in case he should wake up. If he does, I want to be prepared."

"You will be. You will give a fine speech. Come home as soon as you can."

"I will. It's going to be good to see Kate."

We talk another minute, and then we hang up. I think of Kate, the child of our three who is most like me. Twenty years ago, I would not have guessed her life would turn out the way it has, but sometimes a life works out better than even a parent dares to dream, and I think that is the way of Kate's life.

* * *

Rob Nicholson is coming home from his mission. Sam and Ruth have said little about it, but underneath they are bursting with excitement. The joy and anticipation of seeing him again has been held in check, a huge reservoir of feelings swelling behind a dam made of iron will and the notion that all must be given if a sacrifice is complete.

"Anything new from the elder?" I ask them every week.

"Just a little. He's doing fine. Had a baptism last week, and he is teaching a family by the name of Castaneda that he's excited about."

And that is about all they ever say.

But now he is coming home, and their eyes are alight and their movements quick as they prepare to hold their son in their arms. The tears that have been held in check for two years will finally topple over the dam and erupt as a tired, young man in a rumpled white shirt runs toward the airport gate. The flood of emotions will rush home-ward, which is one of the sweetest feelings any of us ever have in this life. Our best and most tender emotions all revolve around home.

Coming home from a mission is part resurrection, part atonement, and part exaltation and symbolizes so much of what we feel as members of this church.

The moment comes, the airplane's wheels touch the tarmac, and the glorious reunion unfolds. Then Elder Nicholson is standing in front of our congregation and bearing his testimony in lyrical Spanish, and not one of us needs a translator because we know what he is saying by the look on his face. His face is, in fact, fuller, the clear eyes blazing. He is more confident. He has become a man of Christ, and his countenance reflects it. He finishes his talk. A counselor moves two seats away, and Rob takes the chair next to his father on the stand.

And sitting to my left is Kate, who listened intently to every word the newly returned missionary spoke.

"He is different now," she says when we are at home and talking about Rob. "I can't say how, but he is different."

In a week, Kate will begin her senior year at BYU. She will graduate in April with a degree in biology. She wants to work in the mountains with wildlife. About her social life we hardly have a clue, other than we know she has broken a few hearts here and there, and she doesn't seem to mind in the least that she is almost ready to graduate and is no closer to marriage than when she arrived at school three years ago. Nor does she seem to fear leaving the university with no prospects of marriage, even though as a society LDS people like to wonder what is "wrong" with a young woman who has reached the ripe, old age of twenty-two or twenty-three and doesn't have a ring on her finger.

They like to say, "Too bad about her. Maybe she should go on a mission. Maybe the Lord has someone in the mission field that she should find."

We love happy, pat, formulaic answers in this church, but life is more complicated than we like to think.

I know this is the case, because I have gone through it much of the way with our daughter Betsy, although she has been taking all of the steps alone the last few years.

Kate still wears her hair long and brown, and I think she is very pretty.

"In what way is he different?" asks Kate's mother.

Kate says, "He is less like a neighbor. Is he going back to BYU?"

And at that moment, whether it is the Holy Ghost at work, father's intuition, or just horse sense, I know that Kate will not be a wildlife biologist in the mountains, putting radio collars on elk or cougars. I know that she will marry Rob Nicholson.

When a father has a moment like this, when he invades territory normally reserved for the females, he wants to blurt out everything at once in a triumphant voice, proving that he too can have inspiration in matters of the heart and not just of the mind and spirit, although I think we males generally do better with the mind part and could use some instruction on the heart part.

I keep quiet, though, because if Rob is the one she should wed, then it must be a discovery of her own. It would not do well years later in a sacrament meeting for her to explain, "Rob and I were neighbors. My father told me before my senior year in college that we would end up married." No, there has to be romance, and my saying what might be so is not very romantic.

I could not contain myself a few nights later, after Kate had left for school and Rob too.

Helen was reading a novel before we went to bed, and I was trying to make my way through Leviticus with little success. I have a feeling that we all will be asked if we have read the standard works fairly early when we arrive in the next life, and I do not want to be embarrassed and have to say, "I read the Book of Mormon, the New Testament, the Doctrine and Covenants, and the Pearl of Great Price many times, but I always got high-centered on Leviticus in the Old Testament." So I was pushing through one of those parts that goes into detail about the coney chewing the cud but not having a divided hoof and still being unclean, the kind of stuff that only Hugh Nibley likes to read, but I could no longer resist telling Helen how smart I was.

"Helen, I have something to say, and it concerns Kate. I think you will be startled and find it very interesting, and your respect for me will grow."

She put aside her book and said, "And what is it that you have to tell me?"

I tried to look profound but couldn't quite capture the aura, and I was making a second run at it when she said, "Are you going to tell me that she and Rob are getting married someday? I already know that."

My attempts at looking profound were instantly replaced by a look of complete befuddlement. "How did you know?" I stammered.

She picked up her book and looked straight ahead and said something that I have no doubt was true. "Women know," she announced, and I got no further with Helen or Leviticus that night.

In September, Kate said she had a date with Rob.

In October, Kate said she'd gone out with someone named Michael from Blanding, but he wasn't very much fun and not all that bright.

In November, Kate said she had a ride home for Thanksgiving with Rob and was glad of it because the trip "wasn't all that far out of the way" for him.

In December, after our Christmas sacrament meeting, Rob, dressed in a white shirt and a red tie and a gray suit, all of which were new since his mission, asked if he could come over and speak to me. I said yes.

"You know what it is for. He is going to ask you about Kate and seek your permission to ask for her hand," Helen said, and I liked the way she said *ask for her hand*.

"They've been out only twice and rode home together once at Thanksgiving and once at Christmas. It is hardly the stuff of an eternal relationship." I spoke from hope, mostly, and not practicality, and I was trying mightily to suppress the revelation I'd received three months before about Kate and Rob.

"Oh, Marcus," she said with a trace of annoyance. "Women know."

"Women talk. That's how they know so much."

To prepare myself for the possibility that a young man was going to ask for the hand of my daughter in marriage, I went to the garage and sat in my car. It was cold, but I had a blanket, and it was quiet and dark. I found myself alone with thoughts like these:

Rob is a returned missionary. He is active and strong and comes from a great family. He will care for Kate and be a good husband and father. He wants to go into medical research, which means many years of school but a good life all in all. He is a nice-looking young man, and because his parents live only a few doors away we will see our children and grandchildren often during the holidays, which is important.

He is kind and generous, and he is no longer much of the clod he was in high school. He is sweet and humble, and he will never hold sway in his home through unrighteous dominion. Yes, all

*things considered, he is a fine young man, and my answer should
be yes.*

I pulled up the blanket over my head, where all was
dark.

But of course, he still isn't good enough for my daughter.

And I got out of my car and came into the house, but
my mind and heart were still at war with each other and
threatening not to take any prisoners.

At seven o'clock sharp, Rob knocked on our door. I
invited him into our living room, which was quiet. I had no
idea where the other members of my household were,
other than I knew they were close by, concerned, and
probably listening to our conversation through the heater
vents.

We sat down, and he looked pale and nervous and
fumbled for words, in stark contrast to his poise when he
spoke in sacrament meeting three months earlier. I
shouldn't have been surprised, because hearts that are
moving and changing can cause havoc and because it
sometimes is difficult to say what you feel.

Eventually he spit out the words, "I would like your
permission and blessing to ask Kate to be my wife," and I
thought he might collapse, and part of me wanted him to.

And at that moment, I looked on top of our piano at a
picture of Kate when she was less than a year old, a picture
fading from age and maybe the thousands of times I had
stared at it. Kate was sitting up, in a white-and-red dress
with two little ducks on the front of it. She had a Santa hat
on, way too large for her, and a teddy bear next to her, also
dressed for the season. Kate's little chin was pointed up,
her dark-brown eyes happy but wondering. Her fingers and
toes were curled, her mouth slightly open, and everytime I
saw this photo of her, I felt that life had endless possibili-
ties and that there was beauty in every direction I looked.

Kate had been ours for twenty-two Christmases, and this picture was part of our every celebration. And I knew, looking at the picture at this moment, what my answer needed to be.

"No, Rob. You cannot have her." At this point, I imagined people near the heater vents falling backward on the floor. "She is mine, and she will be forever, and I never really knew what love was until she came into our hearts." Rob said nothing, trying to figure out what I was going to say next and still hoping that what I said before was a kind of sad joke. "You may ask her to marry you. She will say yes. You are a fine young man, and you are fortunate to have one another. But you cannot have her. At most her mother and I will share her with you, Rob. Good luck, son, and may rich blessings be yours."

I can't remember what I said next or how much longer we talked, but things got a bit lighter and we joked about how long he'd be a student. Then I said, "I will leave now, and you can take her someplace special and have a little talk with her." I called up the stairway and said, "Kate, you have a visitor here, and he wants to talk with you. Better come down, honey."

And when they left a few minutes later, arm in arm, and the door clicked shut, I felt as though something important in my life shut too. Had I been wiser at the time, I would have also recognized that another door was opening, and it led to passages as wonderful as the place where we had been.

In May, we went to the temple with Kate and Rob, Sam and Ruth. Two Decembers later, when we gathered for Christmas, little baby boys, twins, sat in front of the Christmas tree and had their pictures taken. They were dressed in red-and-white outfits and had on little Santa caps.

Their names are Samuel and Marcus. Those little boys are now serving missions, Sam in Ecuador and Marcus in Scotland. Rob got through medical school and ended up in Ann Arbor doing medical research. Kate got her degree in biology and never had much of a chance to use it, other than being the mother of six children, four of them boys; so maybe having training and background in wild, young animals wasn't at all a waste of time.

She often goes camping and hiking with all of her children. I have a picture of them in my mind, a family hiking through a wild mountain meadow, flowers in bloom, sparkling lakes below them in an alpine valley, a mountain ridge ahead to ascend. Two parents with six children in tow. It is a good picture, and I know it is a true picture. It is all so beautiful to me. Without having ever asked, I'm sure Kate and Rob's children know what a swale is and can identify lupine, and that is satisfying and pleasant to think about.

"The kids are coming," Helen said earlier in our phone conversation.

Indeed they are. In some ways, close to my heart, they have never left.

CHAPTER NINE

So the gathering of family members began as Sam's body started to fail and his life became thin and fragile. Perhaps it is an instinct, this desire to gather around as a loved one prepares to depart. Kate would call and ask, "Is it time?" and we would answer, "No, it is not time. Not yet." You balance what the doctors say and what the nurses tell you in private conversations that take place when their professional detachment is waning because you have seen them for days and they have become friends as you all go through a difficult part of life. You look at the one who is ill and think, *No, not yet,* in answer to the terrible question. No, not yet, until the hour comes when something has changed, perhaps almost imperceptibly, and all who are close decide, "Now is the time to gather."

It is a sign of honor, these gatherings. Practical people say, "There is nothing you can do. Stay home. We will take care of things here." But there is something good about seeing a parent or friend before they die. There is something good about prayers that are offered, silent promises that are made, the reflection that comes as farewells are spoken heart to heart and soul to soul. It is a time when close ones probably don't realize how much help they need and the strength that others around them are so willing to give. It is a time when being practical should not be a paramount concern.

Ruth said on Tuesday that it was time to gather, and

the word went forth to the family. Rob and Kate are on their way. The other Nicholson children are coming too. Marcy will come from across town, twenty minutes away. Cynthia and her family will drive from Flagstaff. Jan and Roger will fly from Portland, along with their two eldest children. And David will come from Atlanta. He will travel the farthest of all.

In sacrament meeting, when the speakers drone on, and it is a warm Sunday afternoon, and your thoughts begin to drift pleasantly, sometimes you think, *Oh, there are the Swansons, and they seem to have everything going for them. Their children are perfect, they have no financial concerns, and she is the stake Relief Society president, and he is the high priests group leader. They always have on nice clothes, and they drive a new car every other year. I'm sure they have family prayer at six every morning and they read the Book of Mormon together. They are so perfect I think I am going to be ill.*

We make an error when we compare ourselves to others, and we make an error when we think about the idyllic lives others seem to lead. One of the first lessons I learned after being called to serve as a bishop is that the perfect family does not exist, no matter the outward appearance. We all have problems, we all have challenges, and, because we are reminded so much to be perfect, some families try hard to construct a facade that perfection has been achieved within the walls of their home. I think perfection in this life means that you are a complete person, one who tries hard, endures, repents, forgives, doesn't fudge on tithing, doesn't knowingly do very wrong things, and is nice almost all of the time, and is a good home teacher or visiting teacher to boot.

If I say this aloud in a Gospel Doctrine class, someone will doubtlessly find a scripture or quote Brigham Young and say I am full of hogwash. They might think, *Brother*

Hathaway is a nice old fellow, but his mind has gone around the bend.

Still, I think I am right about this matter of perfection on earth.

And my friend Brigham Young, since he seemed to have thought and said and pondered and philosophized a lot about almost everything, spoke or wrote things that sometimes can be used against you, but it doesn't matter much to me.

Why I'm writing all this is because many people in our stake looked at the Nicholsons through the years and thought they were a family without problems.

I think back. A dozen and a few years ago. Sam and I are walking on the long par-five seventeenth hole at Baybridge. David announced a day ago that he would return to Colorado for his sophomore year in college. But it was more than just saying he would continue his education. It was also a declaration that he would not serve a mission.

"Somehow I hoped it would be different, but in the back of my mind I knew it would not be," laments Sam. "David is a good person. For some reason, the Church never took with him. I always knew where Rob's heart was, but I did not know where David's was. And for a parent, not knowing where your child's heart is always hurts."

Sam has just driven down the fairway, a little to the left. He puts his driver back in his golf bag. "David was elusive and doubtful. I prayed so many times that something would catch hold with him, a person, a talk, a young woman, a lesson, his older brother, Ruth, or me. But it didn't happen. I fear that I will lose him, Marcus."

"You will not lose him, Sam. He has seen too much good in your life and Ruth's life. You will not lose him. Some of that soaks in and is always there, and it will come back to him."

"I hope you are right."

He is now by his golf ball, a three-wood in hand. He squares up to the ball and begins his backswing. It is a warm day in early June, and the earth is at its best. A gentle north breeze brings us the scent of freshly cut grass, flowers in bloom, and hints of a kind and glorious summer ahead.

Sam pushes through his swing, and his golf ball scuzzes a crooked line forty yards to the left. Now I know how upset he really is. I have seen him hit a shot that poorly only once or twice in almost three decades of golfing with him.

"Aw, nuts," Sam fusses.

"It will be okay, Sam."

"If he had just done wrong things, he could repent. It would be so much more simple. He could still have a testimony and repent, and everything would be better. But with David, it is a quiet, intellectual resolve that the Church cannot possibly be what it claims to be, and that is a more terrible enemy than making poor choices and having to repent."

"He'll have to find out some things on his own, and then he will begin to come around. The more experience you have in life, the more the Church rings true. Let him have those experiences, and see if things do not change. He will grab hold, and he will be okay. I feel this is going to be the case, and I would not falsely encourage you. I feel it, Sam."

"Do you?"

"Yes, I do."

Now it is my turn to hit a golf ball. Sam stands back. As if to prove that what I said is true, I blast the ball straight toward the green, which simmers in the sunshine more than two hundred yards away. At this moment, it is confirmed to me that golf is the game of choice in the celestial kingdom.

"Nice shot, pard. Think you're on the frog hair. Got a shot at an eagle, should have a birdie on a gimme," says Sam. "You couldn't have hit a ball like that if you'd just told a lie."

We hole out, and I get my birdie. Sam takes a bogey. He is quiet, still thinking about David. As we stand at the back of the next tee while a foursome ahead of us finishes its drives, Sam asks me quietly, "But why, Marcus? Why is David the way he is? Same parents, same upbringing as the other children, but he is so different."

And there in the shade of a Colorado blue spruce, I think, *Be careful on this one, Marcus Hathaway. What you say is important to Sam, and he will remember it a long while.*

I remember feelings and thoughts such as these when I served as bishop. A man who has been unemployed for eighteen months says he is going to Nevada to work, leaving his family behind, and asks you if it is right. A woman says she is going to divorce her husband and wants to know if she is right. A Primary teacher says that a child in her class of smiling, happy five-year-olds has too many bruises too often. The people who ask these questions are tired and frayed, and they really don't know the answers, and they look at you and want you to just tell them what is right. And you want to help them, but it is not as simple as saying, "Here is the right, and here is the wrong, and if you read this scripture and pray about it, all will be well, and you will be happy, and you will know exactly what to do." Often you do not know what they should do, even with the mantle of a bishop.

Sometimes you can put the decision back on the shoulders of the person who sits across the table from you, but sometimes you cannot and you need to be inspired right then and there, and you hope you are in tune enough that the Holy Ghost will whisper something to you and you will understand, and then they will understand. Then you pray that they'll follow the advice and pray that the Lord will back you up.

Now Sam is placing me in that position with an honest question, an honest heart that is hurting, a father worried about his son, and I want to help. The foursome has finished driving and are marching ahead on the fairway, and Sam expects an answer, so I offer a quick, silent prayer, an occurrence that, in general, is highly unusual on a golf course.

I believe I hear a whisper in my heart, which is where you almost always hear whispers from the Spirit.

"This is what I think, Sam. In the premortal life, you had a heart, which allowed you to love, and you had a mind, which allowed you to make choices. I think your mind recognized in David something that said he might not come home, and you worried about it. And because your heart loved him, you said, 'Send him to me, and let me be his earthly father. I will always love him and teach him and never give up hope, and I will do all I can to help him because I know him so well. I will be patient and kind. He might break my heart many times, and I may lose a thousand nights of sleep over him, but I see him for who he is now and what he may become. So please, send him to me because no one will love him more than I.' You might have said something like that, Sam, and now you have your wish, and your heart is broken and your thousand nights of worry plague your mind, but it could be that you asked for all of this. Maybe it was one of the first decisions entrusted to us, to petition for certain family relationships on earth."

Sam is silent for a moment, then says, "You are profound. Better, you are profound while holding a golf club."

"I am not profound. What I said is taught weekly in Gospel Doctrine classes worldwide. I only said it when you needed to hear it," I tell him.

Sam says, "So it is my own doing? My own fault? You think we could love each other that much without having a body? You have an interesting way of thinking about things."

I say, "I know. Helen tells me that often. And yes, I think much of this is your own doing."

He says, "Do you really think I knew him before?"

I say, "Yes. I think you knew David before and wanted to call him son."

He says, "So I need to love him and teach him and never give up?"

I say, "Yes. That is what I mean, and it is what you would do anyway, but you just needed to hear it from someone else. That's all."

"A thousand nights?"

"Yes. A thousand nights."

It is my turn to tee off. I hit a long, low line drive that kicks up a smatter of dirt when it hits, then runs another fifty yards. It is a good and straight shot. Sam congratulates me, then steps up and hits an almost identical shot, his ball rolling to a stop within a few yards of mine.

"We are together," he says. "We'll let David see a little more of life. Maybe things will change him and he will become less hard about spiritual matters. I feel sorry for anyone who denies their spiritual side. If you don't have a spiritual life, you don't have much."

David never served a mission and for many years never stepped inside one of our churches. He married a young woman named Rebecca, and they had two children. David got into computers early and was a successful businessman. He and Rebecca divorced after eight years of marriage, and during the time of the divorce Sam and Ruth experienced many more of their thousand nights of sleeplessness. Still, David was distant and hard and aloof.

About six months ago, when the seriousness of Sam's illness was becoming apparent, I received an anxious long-distance phone call from David.

"Brother Hathaway," he began, after we had exchanged pleasantries. I was pleased that he called me brother.

"Tell me, how serious is this with my father? I don't think Mother is telling me everything. I think she wants to protect me. Please, just tell me straight out. It's important to me. There are things I need to do, I think."

His voice was warm and caring. It was a different voice than I had heard before from David as we bantered in our front yard about Hegel and Santayana. He was now learning from his experiences, and the spiritual man was coming alive again.

Changes of the heart are still the best of all miracles.

"Your father is very ill," I said, and then gave him the details as I knew them. Over the course of the next few weeks, David became close to his parents again. The thousand nights are almost over for Ruth and Sam.

David and I have stayed in touch these last few months. He is coming today on flight 1286 from Atlanta with a stopover in Salt Lake City. He will arrive at 4:12 P.M.

I am the one who will pick him up. He did not want to add any stress to his mother's life. Ruth thinks he is coming on Sunday.

When I see him, I will stretch forth my thin arms, hug him, and say, "We've missed you, David. Your father loves you. Welcome home."

I think that is exactly what Sam would have done.

* * *

The thin razor of a ridgetop is scarlet, and rosy light floods the higher points of our valley. Somewhere in the journey of the night, the gray clouds were ushered away by unseen windy hands. The hospital sits on a knoll that overlooks the valley. In Sam's room, morning light pierces the thin curtains, and their pattern spreads a warm, gold brocade on the wall. Dawn. *Another dawn, our daily miracle,* I think. All of the stars and moons and suns have come through again, moved in their magical and logical order and conspired to present us with another day. I stand at the window and watch a day unfold second by second as long fingers of orange light streak across the landscape.

Meredith comes in and stands behind me.

"Done for the day," she says. "My day ends when it begins for most others."

"Beginnings and endings run together more when you are old, as I am," I tell her.

"Marcus, you are not old inside. Nor will you ever be."

I hope she is right. Most days, I question my own maturity. Today, were I not so tired, I would like to lick an ice cream cone and sit on a swing in a park. I tell Meredith exactly that.

"Sounds like fun. You'll have a good story to tell about it too."

"Yes, good stories come from experiences, and I try to see stories in much of what I do."

"Has he awakened?"

"No, but I have hope that he will. I have my speech ready and would like to have the chance to deliver it."

"I hope you will be able to talk with him. Anyway, I'm off for a couple of days now. James will be the nurse on duty until late this afternoon. He'll be by soon, I'm sure."

She turns and leaves, and the phone rings.

"Hello, Marcus. I'm so sorry. I was up at four and

thought I would relieve you by six." Ruth speaks quickly, and she sounds distraught. "Then I sat down in the chair and thought I would only close my eyes. The next thing I knew, it was a little after seven and my plan to relieve you had crumpled. Bless you, I'm sure you need a break by now."

"Don't worry, I've had a fine night with Sam. It is unusual for me to do all the talking and him to do all the listening. Sam is mellowing with age," I say, and Ruth laughs, and I feel better because it is always nice to hear someone laugh when they feel sorrowful. "Nothing has changed since you left last night, and I am only a little tired. Come when you can, and in the meantime I will think about stories and may even tell one to your husband. We will be fine."

"Well, thank you. I'll be there before nine. Please call if anything changes, and I will be there in ten minutes. I did sleep a little after midnight, and then the snooze this morning has me wide awake. I feel bad, though. A time like this and I fall asleep. Like Peter in the garden, almost."

"There is no reason for you to feel this way. I can think of only one thing to tell you and that is you are not like Peter in the garden, and what he did wasn't bad anyway. All is well, Ruth."

"Yes, all is well, Marcus. See you soon."

I sit back down in the chair, and its plastic covering squeaks. Ruth's comments about her nap must be more powerful and suggestive than I thought. *I will also close my eyes, just for a few minutes. Then I will stand up and get a bite to eat before she comes.*

My eyelids meet gently, and my thoughts are pleasantly abstract.

And I begin to dream.

"I think it is cancer."

I am sitting in Sam's home in early September, checking up on him because he has not been feeling well and is seemingly unable to shake the chills, the fever, the aches that well up from deep inside.

"Nonsense. You have the flu. You have a virus, and after awhile your body will decide it's had enough of providing a home to a virus, and it will kick the virus out. That's what it is, just a nasty virus that probably got hatched somewhere in Asia."

Sam smiles and looks placid. "Okay, I have the flu, Dr. Hathaway, and I want to kick out the virus right now."

"We'll be on the first tee next Saturday morning."

"Okay. The first tee on Saturday morning."

"So no more mention of the C word, because at our age it is something we should not joke about."

Sam rubs together his hands and sighs. "At our age, we should joke about everything, Marcus. You know that."

And I leave a few minutes later, feeling as though I have been humored.

The next two weeks are a blur, a rising and falling tide of emotions, hopes, and fears. Ruth awaits word from doctors and the results of tests. The doctors seem to be made up of shrugs and puzzled looks and are precious short of answers.

Sam checks into the hospital for a biopsy. The fever doesn't leave.

Inside, I feel that this may be much more than simply a virus that liked the dark, warm, and moist part of Sam, where it made its home.

I am in the hospital with Sam and Ruth and Helen and their youngest child, Marcy, when Dr. Stratford comes in early one evening. We all have been chitchatting, upbeat and happy, while a football game flickers on the TV screen in the corner of the room.

Dr. Stratford looks solemn, but he always looks solemn. I've seen him at wedding receptions, and he looked solemn then too.

"Would you like us to leave?" Helen asks, as it becomes apparent that some answers are now at hand.

"No, I would like you here. You are family too, and I mean it," says Sam, propped up against a pile of pillows and looking calm and comfortable.

Dr. Stratford clears his throat and says, "The news is not very good, Mr. Nicholson. You have prostate cancer, and it looks very much as though it has spread to other areas in your body. We need to talk about surgery and then follow-up treatments, and my inclination is that you will need chemotherapy and radiation. We'll need to get together within the week and outline a strategy. I am sorry, Mr. Nicholson." He pauses, then glances downward and speaks slowly. "Maybe you don't remember me, but I was one of your chemistry students about thirty years ago."

Sam says, "Of course I remember you. Michael Stratford, an A student, always picked up things as soon as I said them. You were quiet and, if I recall, sat about three rows back on the left side. You have less hair now."

Dr. Stratford laughs; Sam has put him at ease. "And you still have all of your hair. You must let me in on the secret. How do you remember all those things?"

"I don't. I remember only the really good students and the really bad students."

"Come and see me next week."

"We'll arrange it. Don't worry, Mike. We will figure out something, and then we will do it, and it will be simple, and we'll hope it works. If not, it's been a nice, long run."

It is time for Sam and Ruth to be alone. Outside in the hallway, Marcy is crying quietly and Helen walks stiffly.

My mind is numb, although I have the sense to stand between them, holding their arms.

It seems as if my world is like a flat winter day in January, when everything is bare and plain and sad. It seems to me, for a second or a little longer, that all the lakes have gone away, there are no more waterfalls, and streams have ceased to run. I think that the flowers and new trees are buried under too much snow deep in the earth, and no amount of warm sunshine will begin their miracle of turning upward and seeking the sky. All I can see in the sky above is a pale, dry moon, and I think that heaven should contain more right now.

It seems to me that life is going too fast, and I feel that something is getting away from me, which is the most disturbing feeling of all, and I don't know what that something is, but it is real and precious. It seems that my feet are made of dark, basaltic stone, and as if in a bad dream I cannot move quickly enough to keep up with what is slipping by me.

And I recognize more than ever that this slippery thing we know as life is a gift with an end and that the only fear any of us should ever have is that we did not live our life the way we should, that we did not immerse ourselves in relationships and pursuing knowledge, opening our arms wide apart and embracing all the wisdom we can, because we will carry it forth and it will help us build our next life too.

And I wonder if we see the Lord everywhere and in everything. I wonder if we fail to appreciate all that is beautiful about us. How much sweetness goes unclaimed in our relentless push to acquire things while beautiful, hidden flowers blush in thin desert air.

And I feel sad and sense that an important part of my life is almost over, but before it is I will witness courage and grace and strength. All of which happened, but this is not a book about a man and his cancer; it is about a man who is my friend and what he taught me.

"I feel sick," says Helen as we hobble down the hallway of the hospital. "I feel so sick inside. I didn't know that our things could come to an end."

Only the thought of Sam's serenity comforts us at this moment.

"Sam was calm, and we should be too," I say.

We walk to Marcy's car. "Will you be okay on the way home?" I ask. She is expecting a baby in three months.

"Yes, I'll be fine. This is a shock, that's all. I hoped for something else, although I didn't believe in anything else. Thank you for being here. Dad couldn't have had better friends to help him with the news," Marcy said.

Outside the hospital room, metal trays clank, and I awaken as orderlies push large racks holding breakfast across the hall.

Sunshine now bathes the room. The last six months have been difficult, but I am glad for what the experience has taught me. My nap is over, but my dream is still fresh. I walk to Sam's bedside. My voice is thick and low, and the back of my throat is sore. My knees ache, and my shoulders are stiff.

"Please, Sam. Wake up. I want to talk with you."

* * *

Sam was released from the hospital the day after the diagnosis, and Helen and I visited him soon after he got settled at home. It was a warm, hazy September afternoon, the kind when the earth is lazy and resting before it expends all it has left by painting the splashy autumn colors.

Sam was glad to be home, and his spirits seemed high.

The Relief Society president and visiting teachers had already come by with casseroles, because that is the way Mormons react to a crisis. If something good happens, you get cookies; if it is sad news, you get casseroles, usually with chicken and cheese. It is as if a hearty chicken-and-cheese casserole will make things better, and when I think about it the sisters are probably right. I'm thankful that tuna casseroles are almost a thing of the past, although I imagine the day will come when someone will say, "We're losing the art of baking tuna casseroles," and, much like quilting clubs, tuna-casserole groups will form all over the Church.

"If there is anything I can do for you, let me know," I said to Sam and Ruth as I stood to leave. This is also part of our LDS culture, to offer to do something for others without being too specific. It always makes us feel good to say it, and then, although we are an honest and sincere people for the most part, we hope they answer something like, "That's okay, we're fine, but thanks anyway," and we can leave with good consciences and a little bit of relief that we weren't asked to shovel snow or drive the car pool for a couple of weeks. "If there is anything I can do for you" ranks high on the list of LDS linguistic icons, right up in the airy neighborhood of "Take us home in safety," "Bless those who couldn't be here this time that they'll come next time," and "I'd like to leave you with my testimony."

But I made the offer to Sam, and we know each other well enough to understand that while the language was trite, the offer was true. He stood at the door as I said it, and instead of graciously declining and saying everything was okay, he thought, then said, "There is one thing, Marcus."

I said, "What is it, Sam?"

And his answer surprised me.

"I would like to go to the mountains once more. I'd like to go up to Cathedral Lakes. I haven't been there for years. My father and I used to hike in there, and it was a beautiful place. Before all those treatments begin and I lose my energy and my hair and before it gets too cold, I'd like to go to the mountains again."

A small part of me started to think, *Well, I don't know. You and I aren't young anymore, and you have a fever and cancer too. It isn't an easy hike into that basin, and at this time of the year we may walk in on a warm day and have six inches of snow the following morning. And you know Ruth and Helen will worry about us the whole time, and they'll think we are just a couple of old men who are trying to relive earlier and better times, and if one of us gets in trouble, the other won't be able to help much. Shouldn't you just stay here and rest and get ready for chemo and think about—*

Think about what? Pain? Good-byes? Death?

I heard myself saying, "Yes, Sam. We need to go to the mountains. If you're up to it, so am I, and we'll have ourselves a nice time. Today is Tuesday, and I can be ready to leave on Thursday. We will stay there one night. I think we'd better come back on Friday, or we'll need the search-and-rescue team to come and get us. Does that sound like a plan?"

"It sounds perfect."

Across the hallway, Ruth and Helen are staring at us as if we are completely mad, but they also have lived with us long enough to understand that this is a pilgrimage and not just another trip to the mountains by two old men.

"Are you sure? Are you going to be okay?" Helen quizzed after we got home.

"Yes, I am sure. We will be okay. Everything will turn out fine. This is my chance to honor the request of a dying

112

man who is a great friend, and I want to do it for him," I reassured, although she wore that expression common to women that says, *If you must, you must, but this is a part of men I do not understand, nor do I care to.*

And so we will be on our way. If something does happen by strange circumstance, if the first fall snow slams high into the mountains and Sam and I are caught in our tent, and by the time the search-and-rescue people get to us we are the color of blue Popsicles and our spirits have departed to a warmer place, I will miss my family and the chance I had to do a few more things and be a part of a few more stories, but I must also add this: Cathedral Lakes, high in a granite cup carved and ground by glaciers, a place where the water is deep-blue and serene and the air is thin and sharp because it is near the top of mountains, is not a bad place to die.

CHAPTER TEN

James walks in. He is a large man, with curly, dark hair and a big, droopy mustache. James is the father of four and used to be in construction, but he wanted to do other things in his life besides argue with subcontractors, so he went back to school when he was in his late thirties and became a nurse.

I like James because I admire anyone who is almost middle-aged and says, "This is not the way I envisioned things turning out, and so I think I'll do something to change the direction of my life." He is a kind and understanding man, and I have enjoyed his company on previous visits to the hospital to see Sam. "I looked at his chart. Not much has changed," he says affably. I cannot visualize him butting heads with sheetrockers.

"I've been here all night, and it has been quiet."

"Not much we can do, is there?" James walks to the bedside. "Makes you wonder what he's thinking or where he is right now. I'm not sure he's really with us."

"Nor am I," I say, making a mental note to sic the missionaries on James one of these days.

"I'll be back later, but if you need me, push the button, holler, or bang on the bedpan, and I'll be here in a flash," he says, straightening up and moving toward the door.

For a moment, it is quiet in the room and hallway. My mind wants to go somewhere else, a place more pleasant.

What was I thinking about? Lost thoughts plague me more than before, another indicator, I fear, of time and age and ability. It was the mountains I was thinking of. Back to Sam in the mountains, to Cathedral Lakes. Yes, that is the place, and my mind wanders back to a balmy September day.

I did all the packing for our last journey to the mountains. I found the old cooking gear for backpacking, the old backpacking tent, the little, collapsible camp stools, the plastic ground cloth, the packs, the sleeping bags, the matches, a small hatchet, and everything else I thought we might need.

Helen and I went to the grocery store and bought food for the trip: two large cans of chili, chocolate bars, bacon and eggs, cookies, fruit juice, ginger ale, little containers filled with peaches, a couple of golden delicious apples, granola bars, and a half-dozen other things. As with most campers, we had about twice as much food as we could possibly expect to eat. That night, we made up peanut butter sandwiches and put them into paper bags. I walked over to Sam's, where Ruth had his clothes packed up. I carefully loaded everything into our station wagon. I told Sam I would pick him up at seven sharp, and we would drive to the trailhead that marked the jumping-off point for Cathedral Lakes.

I felt as excited as a ten-year-old boy on his first backpacking adventure.

"You will be all right, won't you?" Helen asked as we prepared for bed.

"I will be all right. We have enough food to last for days, and we have lots of warm clothing. We are grown men and will not do anything stupid."

"Grown men often do stupid things."

"I know, but we will overcome our natural tendencies

toward committing acts of stupidity, and we'll be fine. I will not let anything bad happen to us on our last trip to the mountains."

She looked at me in a funny way. "You know, don't you? You know Sam is not going to be with us much longer."

"I do know, and that's why I am going to the mountains today. Sam loves them as much as I do. They are beautiful, and when Sam is in pain and when he starts to ebb, he will think of the mountains and our trip to them in September. It will be the best thing for him."

"I'd come with you if you wanted me to, and I know Ruth would also."

"It's okay. You don't need to."

Helen scrunched up her nose and then turned away from me. She was quiet for awhile. I slowly came closer to her and saw that her eyes were filled with tears, and I wondered what she was crying for, but I learned a long time ago that a man must be careful when he asks a woman why she is crying, because if he needs to ask it's probably beyond his understanding anyway, and his question will only increase the flow of tears. So I sat in silence, then snaked my arm around Helen's waist.

"I'm sorry," I finally said, although I didn't know why I said it or why exactly I was sorry. Sometimes men need to just throw out a blanket apology to women, a general plea for atonement, and this was one of those occasions.

"It's okay. I don't like the way I am changing and the way we are changing and the way our friends are changing, but I'd better get used to it. I don't want to be without you, Marcus. I don't want to be alone, and I don't want to feel unneeded. I don't want any more wrinkles, and I want my hair to be long and dark again. I don't want to be old. I don't want to live without you for very long and think of

116

the things I could have done better. I want to see the world as you do, always beautiful, and I want to understand how you see stories in almost everything. I want our children to be little again and us to be strong and young. Do I make sense? Does any of this?"

"Yes, it all makes sense. Our fears are almost always connected to the future and hardly ever with the past, I think. I will come back from the mountains, and we will find stories together and see beautiful things together."

She said, "I love you, Marcus."

I said, "I love you, Helen." And then I pulled her closer to me and kissed her.

She let out a long whoosh of air and leaned back.

"Sam is lucky to have a friend such as you, someone who will take him to the mountains when he is so sick. You are right. He will think often of this trip. You cannot say good-bye and give him better memories than by going with him to the mountains. Just be careful, and don't eat too much chili and drink too much pop, because you are not twelve years old again and your system will play mean tricks on you."

"I will avoid too much pop, and I'll really tone down on the chili," I lied.

We slept well that night. I cannot remember what I dreamed for sure, but I think there were stars and lakes, mountains and waterfalls, and a lean girl of twenty with long and dark hair.

*　*　*

I gently knocked on Sam's door the following morning, a few minutes before seven. He opened the door with a smile on his face. He was dressed in old khaki pants, a fishing vest, short hiking boots, a plaid, flannel shirt, and an ancient fishing hat adorned with all manner of flies.

He looked cute.

"Marcus. Are we set?"

"We are set to conquer the mountains. All you need to do is climb into the car." Ruth appeared behind him in the entryway.

"Make sure you are warm enough. If you get tired, take a rest along the trail. Drink lots of water," she fussed, just before she grabbed Sam's collar and pulled it tight around his neck and gave him a kiss.

It was a little after seven in the morning, and it seemed the whole neighborhood was out to see us off. I'm not sure that someone called around to the people who lived on our street and said, "Sam and Marcus are going to the mountains tomorrow morning. You know how sick Sam is. It would be nice to wave at them as they leave," but it seemed as if everyone was out, from the smallest of the toddlers to the fathers rushing off to work, to the mothers who were either heading to work or stepping outside in their bathrobes, to the teenagers who were running to their cars getting ready to drive to school. We were the center of a small parade, and we waved and smiled at each person we passed.

"This is a nice send-off. I feel like a hero," Sam said, after we turned the corner. I saw him steal a look at the sideview mirror, checking to see if his Ruth was still in their driveway. I looked too, and she was.

I can't recall much about our drive up to the mountains, other than it was a day that seemed to sing. It was warm, with gentle winds that teased and tickled and big, white clouds that looked like dragons blowing across the sky. Sam watched, I do remember, and seemed to be trying to soak in as much as he could. When you are seeing something or doing something for what could be the last time, you draw it in slowly and put your arms around it and lovingly hold it close to you. That is what Sam did on that day last September as we drove higher on curving roads that led us through pine forests, where glassy rivers poured over golden stones and white water thrashed through splintered side canyons.

In silence we drove ahead, although I remember when we curved upward on the road and could first see the mountain peaks that cradled Cathedral Lakes, he said, "I always like hearing the part about the creation in the temple."

"So do I," I said.

About an hour later we were at the trailhead. It was a clearing in the trees with a few places to park and a yellowed Forest Service poster on a bulletin board that told us to be careful with campfires and watch out for bears. I pulled out a map of the area, and we laid it on the hood of our car because that is what men always do when they are about to hike into the mountains. We studied it for a bit and then nodded and said, "This is the way we will go." Then we got our packs out of the car and hefted them on and cinched all of the straps and the belts so that they felt comfortable. We took out our canteens and had a drink of water. I locked the car doors, and we shifted the packs on our backs again, and I said to Sam, "Are you ready?"

He said, "I am ready. I think the trail starts over there. Let's hit it!"

I saw a thin line disappearing among the tall trees, a little path, well worn, its grade climbing up even in the first few feet. I could see the start of the trail but could not see the end, which is much of the intrigue of trails. I was eager to set off, and so was Sam.

We walked a mile. We shed our jackets and tied them onto our packs. We stopped and drank more water. Occasionally we climbed into an opening and could look down below and see how far we had come, which doesn't happen often in life because we think we can see more by looking ahead rather than behind.

We walked another mile, and I could see that Sam was slowing up. "I'm tired. Let's sit on this rock and rest a bit," I said, and Sam wordlessly agreed. We drank water for the third time, then I rustled through my pack and found the sandwiches and granola bars, and we slowly ate them. It was early afternoon, and all I could see was the sky and the mountains and the trees, and it seemed a very good place indeed to eat our lunch.

"Are you feeling rested?" I asked him.

"Yes. I feel fine. I hope to sleep well tonight," he said.

We sat there in the sunshine, and my eyes might have closed. When I opened them, all was blue and swimming and dazzling, and the sky seemed like a great, blue robin's egg above us, and I thought, *The elements know this is our last trip, and there is going to be a show today, because sometimes things work out well, and that will be the way of today.* And so I was not surprised an hour later when the puffy clouds that looked like playful, white dragons became darker and their anvil heads grew black and angry, and I knew it was only a matter of time before they roared and spit out fire.

"Let's get going. I think we are in for a storm late this afternoon. I'd like to have our camp set up before it smacks us," Sam said, almost as if reading my thoughts.

The trail became thinner and the trees smaller and spread farther apart. We were at least two thousand feet above where our car was parked and only a mile from the first link in the chain known as Cathedral Lakes.

Each step was now difficult, and our breath came in short, quick bursts, and for a moment I thought that the women were right and that two old men should not be trying to hike to an alpine lake in September. We came to a huge lip on the side of the mountain, covered with shale and slippery rocks, steep and forbidding, but instead of discouraging us it gave us hope and renewed our spirits. I think it was because we both knew it was our last challenge, and when the end is close by people become stronger, not weaker.

We walked slowly and carefully to the lip, and we held hands in the especially tricky spots, and we finally reached the crest. There ahead of us, like a shimmering piece of sapphire-blue silk, was Little Cathedral Lake, and all we had to do was walk down the slippery shale and set up our camp. "We made it, Marcus," Sam said, and he was pleased with himself.

A few trees crouched on the east end of the lake, and there was a small meadow, but it was mostly a barren place because when we pulled our way to the top of the rocky lip, we were just below the timberline. I told Sam to sit and rest while I put up our tent and arranged our camp. He did not argue, and I went about the business of making camp.

As I did so, the sky blackened more. I had just finished stowing the packs in our tent when Sam said, "Here she comes."

I looked across the small lake and saw the rain line sweeping at us. Thunder bowled our way, so close that it seemed to come from within. Lightning skewered the sky, and I knew the dragon was upon us breathing his humid, hot fire.

And there we were, on the side of a mountain, at the edge of a lake, with the trees swaying from the wind of a dragon's breath.

And it seemed to me an orchestra playing a symphony of wind and sound and flashing light. All seemed in motion, all seemed in rhythm, and the thunder was louder than I ever heard before, and the lightning strikes crackled so close that we could see where they arced their crooked fingers and touched the earth.

I thought, *The lightning is the strings, and the thunder is the big drums, and the wind is the woodwinds, and God in his heaven conducts it all.*

The wind roared like a wounded, wild beast, yet through it all I felt that the dragon was not there to hurt us.

The rain pelted us and whipped our cheeks, and we scurried into the tent, yet we were calm. This was the show, the final show, and Sam knew it, and I knew it, and God knew it, and we knew that this was done for our pleasure and entertainment and our honor. I thought back to the morning, when the children and their parents had saluted us on our way out and felt this too was a tribute to two old men who had always loved the mountains and would not be back again together.

At the height of the storm, when the wind wailed and the rain turned to hail that jumped up and down on the ground, when the lightning looked like a bony hand reaching down to gather us up, when all of this was going on and most people would have hid and prayed for it to be over, Sam stood up outside of the tent and walked to the water's edge and held up his arms high and smiled in his moment of triumph. As the honored guest, he would not be harmed. As the honored guest, he had to acknowledge and accept this final tribute.

I think of him by the lake in the storm and decide that when he is gone and I want to remember him, this is the image I will bring to mind.

The storm boiled around us, and the lake seemed alive, the hail slapping it, the wind fiercely pushing it, and the lightning trying to set the rock and water on fire. It was gorgeous and bold, and I had never seen anything like it.

Then it was over. The curtain dropped, and the orchestra was without its musicians. The slender trees and the grasses of the meadow stopped swaying. The savage hail turned to a trickle of rain, and to the west the sun shyly looked from underneath the last cloud sheet.

Over the lake, near the crest of the highest peak, a double rainbow appeared, and the earth became gentle and timid again.

Sam walked back to me, wet and exultant. "No one will ever believe what we just saw," he said quietly.

"No. No one will. But I will tell this story, and it will be a true story, and they can decide for themselves. But it doesn't matter, because you and I saw it and know it happened."

And a few months later, when the cancer raged and Sam's bones became so brittle that he broke both of his legs by merely getting out of bed, when the pain was relentless and unforgiving, when his tongue was thick and his eyes were wild and his skin turning yellow, this is the moment that he remembered, and no man anywhere could have asked for a better farewell from the mountains than he and I experienced at Little Cathedral Lake.

The texture of the sky changed from rough, dark wool to silk, and the sun was going down, weary from another day of work. All of the parts of our surroundings now seemed tranquil, and the fragrance from the onion grass in the meadow gently crept our way. Little meadow marigolds peeped out from the cover of damp Idaho fescue. The dark dragon had visited, and fire came from his mouth, but all had survived, and now all was peaceful.

I pulled out the cookstove and placed the canister of fuel underneath. I poured the chili out of the two cans and placed the pan on the burner. I reached into my backpack and got two cans of ginger ale and two chocolate bars. Soon the chili was bubbling, and I spooned it out. Sam set up our two camp stools, and we had our dinner before us. I have eaten many meals in the mountains, but the chili and ginger ale and chocolate bars that I ate that night with Sam may have been the best meal I ever partook of under the stars.

We talked between spoonfuls of chili.

I said, "The storm this afternoon was all for you."

He said, "I know it was. It was a good storm."

I squirmed a bit because I wanted to talk with him about something but wondered if it might seem silly now.

I said, "When we were younger, we used to talk about things that would happen when we got older."

He said, "Yes. Do you mean about becoming fine old high priests?"

I nodded my head and took another big bite of chili.

It was dark, and I could not see the face of my friend very well. He grew silent, but I knew what he was thinking, which can happen when you've known someone for forty years.

He was thinking of fine old high priests.

He was thinking that although it never will be found in the scriptures and although a man could never be ordained a fine old high priest, it is an office that nonetheless exists.

A fine old high priest is someone who has wavy, white hair, if he has hair at all, or he has thin, strandy hair that long ago faded to gray. A fine old high priest wears gold-rimmed glasses and works in the temple and without being asked puts back the hymnbooks in the chapel. He is a person who sees gentleness more clearly than ever before, and it is the hallmark of all he does. A fine old high priest's words are always kind and loving. He thinks nothing is better than to have a child sit on his lap, unless it is to watch a baby fall asleep in his arms. A fine old high priest knows there is more to be gained from life by slowing down than by speeding up. A fine old high priest holds his wife's hand when they walk together toward church and still thinks she is the most beautiful woman in the world. A fine old high priest believes snow is a miracle and waterfalls are too. A fine old high priest doesn't care about gain or getting ahead or making money or who is right and who is wrong but concerns himself more with finding wisdom. A fine old high priest is at peace with himself, and he understands life, and he knows he can't tell another how to become a fine old high priest because it is something that is not sought but happens gradually and may take a lifetime or more. A fine old high priest finds joy in common things, treasures a crayon drawing from a five-year-old more than any piece of art in a museum, and nothing bothers him much because he knows that he has done well and this part of existence is almost over and he needs only to endure another season. A fine old high priest knows how to say good-bye and looks forward to saying hello. A fine old high priest likes where he is in the world he created.

Many men grow old, and many are high priests. It is the fine part that is difficult to attain.

I think that Brigham Young and Joseph Smith know what a fine old high priest is, and I think if I could ask our prophet today, "Do you know what a fine old high priest is?" he would smile and say yes, and no further explanation would be needed.

I could see only the bare outline of Sam, and he was very still.

"Are we fine old high priests now?" I asked, and as I stated the question my breath stopped short and my heart started to race and I felt a prickly sensation up and down my back, and I knew his answer would be true.

"Yes, we are fine old high priests," came the voice in the dark.

"I think so too."

And I was happy at that moment, sitting near the edge of the lake with the slim cut of the moon rising in the eastern sky over the top of the cirque that held the lake. The air was still and cold, and every word we said seemed to hang in the night and become solid, almost as if the words turned to stone and I could put them in my pocket and hold them in days to come.

"I think I'll turn in now," Sam said.

"I will too. I am tired. Two old men in the mountains, our last chance to stay up late and eat more chili and tell stories, and it's only 8:30, and we're both exhausted and want to turn in," I teased. "Do not tell Ruth and Helen. Tell them instead we stayed up late and told good stories and laughed so hard we cried ourselves to sleep."

"Okay. But this is my last night in the mountains, and I may not sleep at all, or I may cry myself to sleep out of sadness, I don't know."

"Either way is okay, Sam."

"Good night, Marcus."

I cleaned up the camp and took my flashlight and walked to the edge of the still, dark lake. I shined my flashlight into the thick darkness but could not see the other side of Little Cathedral Lake. I thought, *This is a dark lake, and I think I know what is on the other side because I saw it before and it looked very beautiful, but I will not yet cross the lake. Sam will cross it before me, and I will stay on the shore and wave to him, and I will put my arm around Ruth, and we will all miss him, but he knows it is time to complete the journey.*

And I thought some more: *When I leave this side of the lake and reach the other, I think I will feel relieved in many ways. I think I will be glad for the experiences I've collected and the chance to be here for a while, but I think I will be happy to come home and not have to go through all of this again, even though most of it has been good. It is still a hard journey, and there is danger in every step of the way.*

Then I became tired too, and I walked the few yards up to the tent and rolled out my sleeping bag. I think that Sam was already asleep, and I am glad that he did not cry himself to sleep because no man should ever cry himself asleep on his last night in the mountains.

Across the lake, I thought I saw a light shining, although I did not know any other backpackers were on the trail. It was a steady, white light, just a dot, and I could not hear any voices, but it gave me comfort to know that we were not alone high in the mountains at the edge of a dark lake that night.

The following morning when we arose before dawn, I looked across the lake to find out who our neighbors might be, and I listened for their voices.

But there were no voices or any sign of campers and the clear white light never appeared again.

*   *   *

"The sun will be coming up soon. Let's watch the sun rise."

Sam was gently nudging me, and his voice was excited.

"The sun. We can't be up here and not greet the day."

My body ached, and I shivered, and I had not slept very well. My fingers felt like ten pieces of crooked stone, and the air beyond my sleeping bag was harsh and biting.

"Let's greet the day," Sam insisted.

I sat up in my sleeping bag and then pulled myself out of it. I fumbled for my outer clothing in the thick, blue darkness before sunrise. I stood up, still hunched over in

127

our small tent, then stepped outside, where Sam awaited me. I pulled out my sleeping bag, unzipped it, and used it as a shroud to shield me from the thin, icy air of morning. The lake was dark and the ridge behind it black and brooding.

Sam had our camp stools in hand and was walking vigorously toward the small meadow behind our tent. He stopped once and looked behind to make sure I was following. In the murky light of a morning hardly touched by sunlight, I could see the excitement in his face at being in the mountains for a sunrise.

And from him, I understood this:

When it is quite possibly your last chance to see the sun rise in the mountains, you must take advantage of the opportunity and savor every second.

Sam set up the camp stools. They faced east, where the sun would soon peer over the tall shale ridgeline where Sam and I had crossed over a saddle and dropped into the bowl of Little Cathedral Lake only yesterday afternoon. He motioned for me to sit down, and I did so. We sat in silence and waited for the drama of a new day's start.

First the sky began to lighten, a line of crimson, then gold. The ridgeline became more distinct as the light seeped into its cuts and crags and revealed its character.

Most often, I think, when things begin to change, they start with light.

Then came the cirrus clouds, ribbed and wispy, warmed in the rosy glow. Their undersides caught the first light and turned pink, their deeper canyons clinging to purple and black. Then all the clouds became lighter, and we could see them stretching from the southwest to the northeast, following a high, windy road. The sun broke over the ridgeline, and we strained to absorb its feeble warmth. On the higher ridges of the cirque to the west, I could see a dusting of snow. It was the most beautiful sight I have ever seen in the mountains.

Sam and I sat frozen in awe and said nothing to each other.

In my mind, I heard the strains of Beethoven's "Pastoral."

Our high lake valley then filled with sunshine.

Sam finally spoke. "That was a sunrise."

"Yes. I feel that there is a story here, and I am lucky to be a part of it. The best stories are those that you are part of."

He said, "You love stories, don't you?"

I said, "I do. I remember stories best, and I learn the most from stories."

He said, "You are a fine storyteller, but you also need to write them."

I said, "I am not a writer. I cannot write. How do you write?"

He said, "You write what you feel, and the voice you use is the voice you talk with. All good stories that are written begin with a feeling."

I knew what he was trying to tell me. So I said, "You want me to write about being in the mountains with my old friend who is sick, and you want me to write about our lives and what we now know of friendship."

He nodded. "Yes, I do. I know you can write about all of that."

So sitting on a camp stool, no longer cold, Sam and I had the conversation that was the beginning of this book. It is why, when I am seventy-one years old, I am trying to write a book, even though I can't remember all the words I once knew, and I must think harder about how I want to say things, and my fingers ache after I sit at the keyboard for more than a half-hour, because of my arthritis. And when I get discouraged and think no one will ever want to read my stories, I think about Sam and me on our camp stools near the lake and, in so many words, how he told me to write this story and the other stories of my life. Then I remember the feelings I had and have, and the words come back to me, and sometimes they come so quickly that I cannot type fast enough to keep up with the flow. Sam was right. Stories, I think, always begin with a feeling.

"Okay. I will write the story, and you can edit it. You're the schoolteacher, remember. Is that a fair proposition?"

Sam stared ahead to the edge of the lake and the shale cliffs above it.

"I won't be around for the editing, and you know it, and I know it. This is your project, Marcus, and you need to finish it."

I did not like what he said, even though I also knew he wouldn't be around. Just because you know such things and feel such things when you are old, and you understand when your body says that it is enough and that your time is almost at hand, it still doesn't mean that you like to talk about what is ahead.

I said with falseness, "Nonsense. You will dance on my grave and check up on Helen every other day. You will shoot par at least three more times after I am growing lilies on my chest."

He ignored me. "When I die, I want you to speak at my funeral, and I want you to tell our stories."

"I will do no such thing. You will speak at my funeral."

He ignored me again. "You will speak, and I would like to hear those stories. You don't know how much I've loved listening to you tell stories all these years. I never told you. You know the stories of my life better than any-one except Ruth, and I don't expect she'll much feel like telling them at that time. I'm counting on you for this."

I didn't say anything because I could see that I had traveled up a canyon that ended in a tall, rock slope that was not possible to climb out of. So I said to myself, *Fine. If he dies first, I will speak at his funeral, and I'll tell stories about him. If he dies first, Sam will have won this round from me. He is a stubborn man, not at all like me.*

We sat in silence for a few more minutes. After you have spoken of things that are difficult, sometimes it is best to not say anything and to sit in silence.

Sam stood up. The sun warmed the whole lake basin and washed it clean.

"I will go fishing now," he said. "Do you want to join me?"

"Sure, but I'd like to fish the other end of the lake, and you can stay on this side."

He said, "All right."

We walked slowly back to the tent, and we got our gear and outfitted ourselves. He walked toward the east, and I walked toward the west. I had my rod but really didn't want to fish much; I really wanted to watch Sam.

I was about fifty yards away from him when he began his first cast. I saw the air sliced methodically and beautifully, the line in wavy arcs over his head, his eyes on the lake. Sam was a purist and used a fly even on a lake. He had walked out on a slim, rocky ledge that dropped into a deep pool of dark water. There was magic in that moment as the sunlight cradled and swathed Sam and in the perfect rhythm in which he moved his arm and cast his line.

And I thought of what boys had said about him for forty years: "He thinks like a fish."

I fiddled with my own gear for a few minutes and then sat on a rock. Sam was absorbed in fishing, and for a moment in the dazzling sunlight, watching an artist at work with his rod in hand, everything seemed so right and perfect, and I somehow hoped that the giant hand of the priesthood would nestle upon him, and he would be spared for awhile longer, and perhaps this was not our last trip to the mountains. I hoped in one bright moment that the cells that were dividing unchecked in his body and taking away the life of the vital cells would cease their multiplying and that Sam's life would be maintained. I hoped this but knew it was not meant to be.

I watched him for perhaps fifteen minutes. I gradually moved closer to him. I thought he might look up at me and wave, but he was enraptured by the rod and the line and the water and the breaking day. I put down my rod and felt as though I were sharing a secret with him: his last trip to the mountains, his last time fishing, and of course the last fish he ever caught.

It wasn't a big fish. That high in the mountains, in a small lake, fish don't grow to be very big, but it might have been his finest fish because it was his last fish. I saw the fish jump at the fly and the slow arc spread, then the furious wiggling and splashing, the fight for life, one dying creature linked to another. Sam moved his arms methodically, rocking slightly, pulling up the rod, reeling in line, then letting it go slack for a moment. The fish, drained of energy, fought less, and soon Sam was bending down with his rod arched high over his head and a little net in his left hand and pulling the fish toward him. Sam caressed the little fish, which was not more than ten or eleven inches I'd guess, and removed the hook from his mouth. He laid down his rod on the stony shelf behind him and gracefully knelt toward the water. He swayed his hands in the water and then lifted his fingers away, and the tired fish lolled for a moment and then darted back into the dark water.

Now there was only one dying creature at the lake.

It was done. Sam never again cast a line into water.

When Sam is gone and I am missing him, at the times when I would like to walk over to his home and talk with him, when I'd love to walk with him up a fairway during a spring so alive that you can almost feel it breathe and hear its heart beating, when I would like to talk with him about my Betsy and about a life that sometimes feels hollow, when I wake from a deep sleep in the black hours beyond midnight and realize that my good friend is gone, I think I will picture him as he was in that moment: kneeling at the lakeside, swaying, a little cutthroat trout swimming toward cold, dark waters and freedom.

I suppose this is where a certain part of a story began to end. A good storyteller knows when stories begin, and he knows where they are going when he is telling them, and he knows when they end. A good storyteller also knows to never say more than is really in the story.

Two hours later, we were back on the trail, this time headed down the mountain. We were home by four, when the lazy, late afternoon sun seemed to coat everything in light orange and dust. Ruth and Helen spilled through the Nicholsons' doorway to greet us, and once assured that all was well we decided to go out for dinner that night, for Italian food at a little restaurant called Johnnie's, a place where we knew the owner and the food was good and we were always served dessert at no extra cost.

We all said good night to each other on Sam's driveway, our arms locked together, trying to hold on to the moment, when we could look the other way for a few more minutes and pretend that we didn't see a large and angry cloud blowing our way.

Chapter Eleven

Peter was right: your old men dream dreams. I dream more now than I used to. You think of dreams, and you connect them with childhood, or you think of young men and young women who see a passionate world ahead of them, and they dream of it all being at their feet someday.

But I know now that old people dream more than others and that their dreams are good and their dreams are true, because all of the pretense is gone. The world doesn't glisten with passion as it did when you were young, but the world is more gentle, and that makes it a better place. What they dream about often has already happened, and that makes their dreams tangible, good memories recalled.

I shake my head and rub my hands across my forehead. It is a little after nine, and I thought that Ruth would have arrived by now. My stomach growls, and I can smell breakfast and hear the clatter of trays from nearby rooms. I get up and stretch my arms high above my head and groan. I walk outside the room and head toward a vending machine.

I find two quarters in my pocket and insert them in the machine. I pull back the plastic window and put my fingers around a small carton of milk.

What now? I think. My day is almost ending; my day is almost beginning. What lies ahead? Ruth probably will be in the room when I get back.

I walk ahead slowly, feeling tired and encumbered.

What next? What next? I think over and over. When you are old, you need to be needed, and I am unsure of how needed I am. I have only things to do today, good things, yes, but things nonetheless. And doing things and being needed are not the same. Perhaps it is because of exhaustion and the drain of the night and maybe it is partly just a function of my age, but I feel anxiety at the thought that I have little time left myself, and I worry that my life is no longer a part of many peoples' stories.

And I fret.

Wearily I push open the door to Sam's room. Ruth is not here yet. I look at Sam. My carton of milk plops to the floor.

His eyes are open.

And I know what comes next.

It is time for my speech.

I walk over to him quietly and quickly. I do not want to startle him. I feel as though I am approaching a timid child and not my friend of almost five decades. I reach his bedside. His eyes are moving rapidly, and I feel that he is trying to make sense of his situation.

He notices me. I am not sure he recognizes me. He moves his lips as if to speak, but words do not come. I place my right hand on him and gently rub his forehead. His eyes steady, and he stares at me.

Oh, Sam. How I wish things were different. My brother, our Sam.

I lean over and kiss him on his cheek.

It is time for my speech. I do not know how much longer his eyes will remain open, and it seems critical to me that I talk to him while he can see. I take a deep breath and run my hand across his forehead again. I kneel and put my mouth close to his ear.

And then I give the best speech of my life, the best

because it is short and true and it is exactly what I mean and it comes from my heart.

"We are friends, Sam. Fine old high priests who are fine old friends."

He does not speak, nor does he move. Instead he closes his eyes. And I feel peaceful, and I have not worried so much or felt quite as alone or as unneeded since then.

And for the third time in my adult life I weep, but the tears are not tears of sorrow.

I know that Sam is done with one part of his life and that his was a good story. I know that he accomplished all that he was sent and meant to do.

Ruth walks into the room. "I'm sorry, Marcus. I just can't seem to move very fast." Then she sees my tears. "Is he okay? Are you okay?"

"Yes, he is still with us. I am okay. He opened his eyes a few minutes ago, and I was able to talk with him. Ruth, I know he heard me, and I know he understood."

And Ruth's eyes swell and moisten. "Yes, yes he did. I'm sure of it, Marcus."

"He will open his eyes for you too. I know he will. You will be the last one for whom he opens his eyes."

She turns away from me and takes a few steps, her exercise shoes squeaking on the floor. She looks at the window.

"I hope so."

She looks at me over her left shoulder. "I suppose we should show a little more faith, shouldn't we? Sometimes faith seems to slip away. You have to work to keep faith, don't you. There's more to the scripture about faith and works than most of us think."

"There is. But your faith is fine. It has been tested and bent, but it never broke."

I gather up my coat and turn toward the door. "Let me

know if you need anything. Helen and I will be here quickly if something changes."

"Thank you, Marcus. Thank you so much. We are friends, aren't we?"

"Yes, we are friends and will be always."

I leave the room and walk to the nurses' desk. James is there, filling out forms. "Done for the day?"

"Yes, I think so. May I use the phone here? I spent my last quarters on some milk, and then it spilled on the floor. I want to call my wife and let her know I'm coming home. I imagine she is worried about me."

"Go right ahead. Dial nine to get out. Yeah, I'm sure your wife is worried. They're made that way."

"Thank you, James. Yes, women worry a lot. It's one of the things I like about them."

I dial the phone number to my house. Helen answers. She also sounds tired.

"I'm on my way home. Ruth just now got here."

"I'm glad that you are coming home. You need to rest. I'll have some breakfast on the table, and then you need to get to bed. You're not a young man anymore, Marcus. Can't burn the candle on both ends at your age."

"A cliché that I know to be true."

"Is Sam okay?"

"Yes. Not much change. He did wake up for a minute this morning." I pause. "I gave him a speech, Helen. It was a very fine speech. I think he understood. I think it was meant to be that I was there when he opened his eyes, and I was meant to give him that speech. I'm glad that I stayed with him last night."

"It's good that you had the chance to share your speech with him, Marcus. Tell me about it over breakfast. What else do you have planned for today?"

"Well, I have important things to do. I'm going to pick

up David at the airport. Ruth and Sam don't know he's coming in, and he didn't want to trouble them. So I'll do that a little after four. And then there is Betsy. I want to take her out for lunch or dinner tomorrow. It will be Saturday, so we can do that. I've thought a lot about Betsy, and I want to do more with her. She needs her father."

"Yes, she does, but you'll have to get in line. See, Marcus, she's going out tomorrow with a young man by the name of Mark Chambers. He's divorced. They met about a month ago at one of those singles conferences. He has two small children. He is a schoolteacher."

"A schoolteacher? Two schoolteachers. They have a lot in common."

"Yes. Now I don't want you to get excited, even though you always do. Betsy will make her own choices. We can't live her life for her or make her decisions. So don't interfere. And don't get carried away. You get carried away too much. You really do. You've probably already envisioned a scene at the temple and getting our backyard ready for a reception."

I say, "I have. But Betsy is beautiful. Don't you think our daughter is beautiful?"

She pauses for a moment, and when she answers her voice is thick. "Yes, our daughter is beautiful. And you are beautiful too, Marcus."

I say, "But I am a skinny, old man. You said I was best when I was about twenty-eight and you hoped that when I was resurrected that's the age I'd be. Now you are saying that I'm not too bad, beautiful even, and I am seventy-one. This confuses me."

Helen giggles. "I'm confused too. We are confused together. I'm glad we are confused together. I don't feel so alone."

"We need to make sure we don't get so confused that

they put us in an institution together."

"Come to your home, Marcus. Come now. You make my world warm when it sometimes seems to be growing cold."

I put down the phone and feel content.

"Everything okay at home?" asks James.

"Yes. Everything is well, just as it should be."

"Always a nice feeling to know that."

"I will probably see you again, James. Take good care of my friend and his wife."

"I will, Marcus. My medical opinion for you is that you should get some rest."

"You and my wife are part of a wide-ranging conspiracy. I promise to be in bed within an hour and having nice dreams."

I walk past the elevator and down one flight of stairs. I walk around a corner and down a hallway. I stand at the corner where the glass meets in the maternity ward. My little, pink friend Harold is gone. A nurse stands by, a question in her eyes. But our society is more tolerant of old, eccentric people, so she only listens curiously as I speak.

"I am sorry I missed you, Harold. I wish for you the chance to soar in this life. My thought is that you will. May you safely find your way home, Harold."

The nurse walks away, and so do I. I pick my way down two more flights of stairs and push through a door into brilliant sunshine. The sun warms me and lulls me at the same time. The air is sweet. The clouds of last night have disappeared, and it seems to me that the earth has awakened and a million blossoms will burst forth this day. The mountains wear a fine cape of new snow, but all around me brown is being left behind and the new face of the earth is a pale, fresh green.

And I think about hope and faith and the sense that all is in order and all will turn out well, and I think that we are not as far from God as we most often believe, even when we can't see much ahead. I think, *Roads have an end, but journeys do not, and I know I am on a journey, as we all are.*

I am an old man. Better, a fine old high priest who is still strong and has a purpose.

I am needed, and I cannot think of anything better for someone my age.

I have a talk to write about a friend and a story to tell.

And my question at the beginning is answered by all that is about me: The people I love, the lives they live, the blue, solemn mountains above me, the flowers that will soon break through the fine crust of soil below me, and most of all the beliefs I possess.

It is not winter. It is spring. A good and gracious and sweet spring that will last always and always.